HAIRCUT AND OTHER STORIES

By Ring Lardner

THE BEST SHORT STORIES OF RING LARDNER

YOU KNOW ME AL

HAIRCUT

AND

OTHER STORIES

by Ring Lardner

COLLIER BOOKS
Macmillan Publishing Company
New York

Maxwell Macmillan Canada
Toronto
Maxwell Macmillan International
New York   Oxford   Singapore   Sydney

Collier Books   Maxwell Macmillan Canada, Inc.
Macmillan Publishing Company   1200 Eglinton Avenue East
866 Third Avenue   Suite 200
New York, NY 10022   Don Mills, Ontario M3C 3N1

Macmillan Publishing Company is part of the
Maxwell Communication Group of Companies.

Library of Congress Cataloging-in-Publication Data
Lardner, Ring, 1885–1933.
    Haircut and other stories / by Ring Lardner.—1st Collier Books
ed.
       p.   cm.
    ISBN 0-02-022344-7
    I. Title.
    [PS3523.A7H3   1991]   91-15748   CIP
813'.52—dc20

First Collier Books Edition 1991

10 9 8 7 6 5 4 3 2 1

Printed in the United States of America

CONTENTS

HAIRCUT AND OTHER STORIES

HAIRCUT

I got another barber that comes over from Carterville and helps me out Saturdays, but the rest of the time I can get along all right alone. You can see for yourself that this ain't no New York City and besides that, the most of the boys works all day and don't have no leisure to drop in here and get themselves prettied up.

You're a newcomer, ain't you? I thought I hadn't seen you round before. I hope you like it good enough to stay. As I say, we ain't no New York City or Chicago, but we have pretty good times. Not as good, though, since Jim Kendall got killed. When he was alive, him and Hod Meyers used to keep this town in an uproar. I bet they was more laughin' done here than any town its size in America.

Jim was comical, and Hod was pretty near a match for him. Since Jim's gone, Hod tries to hold his end up just the same as ever, but it's tough goin' when you ain't got nobody to kind of work with.

They used to be plenty fun in here Saturdays. This place is jam-packed Saturdays, from four o'clock on. Jim and Hod would show up right after their supper, round six o'clock. Jim would set himself down in that big chair, nearest the blue spittoon. Whoever had been settin' in that chair, why they'd get up when Jim come in and give it to him.

You'd of thought it was a reserved seat like they have sometimes in a theayter. Hod would generally always stand or walk up and down, or some Saturdays, of course, he'd be settin' in this chair part of the time, gettin' a haircut.

Well, Jim would set there a w'ile without openin' his mouth only to spit, and then finally he'd say to me, "Whitey,"—my right name, that is, my right first name, is Dick, but everybody round here calls me Whitey—Jim would say, "Whitey, your nose looks like a rosebud tonight. You must of been drinkin' some of your aw de cologne."

So I'd say, "No, Jim, but you look like you'd been drinkin' somethin' of that kind or somethin' worse."

Jim would have to laugh at that, but then he'd speak up and say, "No, I ain't had nothin' to drink, but that ain't sayin' I wouldn't like somethin'. I wouldn't even mind if it was wood alcohol."

Then Hod Meyers would say, "Neither would your wife." That would set everybody to laughin' because Jim and his wife wasn't on very good terms. She'd of divorced him only they wasn't no chance to get alimony and she didn't have no way to take care of herself and the kids. She couldn't never understand Jim. He *was* kind of rough, but a good fella at heart.

Jim and Hod had all kinds of sport with Milt Sheppard. I don't suppose you've seen Milt. Well, he's got an Adam's apple that looks more like a mushmelon. So I'd be shavin' Milt and when I'd start to shave down here on his neck, Hod would holler, "Hey, Whitey, wait a minute! Before you cut into it, let's make up a pool and see who can guess closest to the number of seeds."

And Jim would say, "If Milt hadn't of been so hoggish, he'd of ordered a half a cantaloupe instead of a whole one and it might not of stuck in his throat."

All the boys would roar at this and Milt himself would force a smile, though the joke was on him. Jim certainly was a card! There's his shavin' mug, settin' on the shelf, right next to

Charley Vail's. "Charles M. Vail." That's the druggist. He comes in regular for his shave, three times a week. And Jim's is the cup next to Charley's. "James H. Kendall." Jim won't need no shavin' mug no more, but I'll leave it there just the same for old time's sake. Jim certainly was a character!

Years ago, Jim used to travel for a canned goods concern over in Carterville. They sold canned goods. Jim had the whole northern half of the State and was on the road five days out of every week. He'd drop in here Saturdays and tell his experiences for that week. It was rich.

I guess he paid more attention to playin' jokes than makin' sales. Finally the concern let him out and he come right home here and told everybody he'd been fired instead of sayin' he'd resigned like most fellas would of.

It was a Saturday and the shop was full and Jim got up out of that chair and says, "Gentlemen, I got an important announcement to make. I been fired from my job."

Well, they asked him if he was in earnest and he said he was and nobody could think of nothin' to say till Jim finally broke the ice himself. He says, "I been sellin' canned goods and now I'm canned goods myself."

You see, the concern he'd been workin' for was a factory that made canned goods. Over in Carterville. And now Jim said he was canned himself. He was certainly a card!

Jim had a great trick that he used to play w'ile he was travelin'. For instance, he'd be ridin' on a train and they'd come to some little town like, well, like, we'll say, like Benton. Jim would look out the train window and read the signs on the stores.

For instance, they'd be a sign, "Henry Smith, Dry Goods." Well, Jim would write down the name and the name of the town and when he got to wherever he was goin' he'd mail back a postal card to Henry Smith at Benton and not sign no name to it, but he'd write on the card, well, somethin' like "Ask your wife about that book agent that spent the afternoon last week," or "Ask your Missus who kept her from gettin' lonesome the last time you was in Carterville." And he'd sign the card, "A Friend."

Of course, he never knew what really come of none of these jokes, but he could picture what *probably* happened and that was enough.

Jim didn't work very steady after he lost his position with the Carterville people. What he did earn, doin' odd jobs round town, why he spent pretty near all of it on gin and his family might of starved if the stores hadn't of carried them along. Jim's wife tried her hand at dressmakin', but they ain't nobody goin' to get rich makin' dresses in this town.

As I say, she'd of divorced Jim, only she seen that she couldn't support herself and the kids and she was always hopin' that some day Jim would cut out his habits and give her more than two or three dollars a week.

They was a time when she would go to whoever he was workin' for and ask them to give her his wages, but after she done this once or twice, he beat her to it by borrowin' most of his pay in advance. He told it all round town, how he had outfoxed his Missus. He certainly was a caution!

But he wasn't satisfied with just outwittin' her. He was sore the way she had acted, tryin' to grab off his pay. And he made up his mind he'd get even. Well, he waited till Evans's Circus was advertised to come to town. Then he told his wife and two kiddies that he was goin' to take them to the circus. The day of the circus, he told them he would get the tickets and meet them outside the entrance to the tent.

Well, he didn't have no intentions of bein' there or buyin' tickets or nothin'. He got full of gin and laid round Wright's poolroom all day. His wife and the kids waited and waited and of course he didn't show up. His wife didn't have a dime with her, or nowhere else, I guess. So she finally had to tell the kids it was all off and they cried like they wasn't never goin' to stop.

Well, it seems, w'ile they was cryin', Doc Stair came along and he asked what was the matter, but Mrs. Kendall was stubborn and wouldn't tell him, but the kids told him and he insisted on takin' them and their mother in the show. Jim found this out afterwards and it was one reason why he had it in for Doc Stair.

Doc Stair come here about a year and a half ago. He's a mighty handsome young fella and his clothes always look like he has them made to order. He goes to Detroit two or three times a year and w'ile he's there he must have a tailor take his measure and then make him a suit to order. They cost pretty near twice as much, but they fit a whole lot better than if you just bought them in a store.

For a w'ile everybody was wonderin' why a young doctor like Doc Stair should come to a town like this where we already got old Doc Gamble and Doc Foote that's both been here for years and all the practice in town was always divided between the two of them.

Then they was a story got round that Doc Stair's gal had throwed him over, a gal up in the Northern Peninsula somewheres, and the reason he come here was to hide himself away and forget it. He said himself that he thought they wasn't nothin' like general practice in a place like ours to fit a man to be a good all round doctor. And that's why he'd came.

Anyways, it wasn't long before he was makin' enough to live on, though they tell me that he never dunned nobody for what they owed him, and the folks here certainly has got the owin' habit, even in my business. If I had all that was comin' to me for just shaves alone, I could go to Carterville and put up at the Mercer for a week and see a different picture every night. For instance, they's old George Purdy—but I guess I shouldn't ought to be gossipin'.

Well, last year, our coroner died, died of the flu. Ken Beatty, that was his name. He was the coroner. So they had to choose another man to be coroner in his place and they picked **Doc**

Stair. He laughed at first and said he didn't want it, but they made him take it. It ain't no job that anybody would fight for and what a man makes out of it in a year would just about buy seeds for their garden. Doc's the kind, though, that can't say no to nothin' if you keep at him long enough.

But I was goin' to tell you about a poor boy we got here in town—Paul Dickson. He fell out of a tree when he was about ten years old. Lit on his head and it done somethin' to him and he ain't never been right. No harm in him, but just silly. Jim Kendall used to call him cuckoo; that's a name Jim had for anybody that was off their head, only he called people's head their bean. That was another of his gags, callin' head bean and callin' crazy people cuckoo. Only poor Paul ain't crazy, but just silly.

You can imagine that Jim used to have all kinds of fun with Paul. He'd send him to the White Front Garage for a left-handed monkey wrench. Of course they ain't no such a thing as a left-handed monkey wrench.

And once we had a kind of a fair here and they was a baseball game between the fats and the leans and before the game started Jim called Paul over and sent him way down to Schrader's hardware store to get a key for the pitcher's box.

They wasn't nothin' in the way of gags that Jim couldn't think up, when he put his mind to it.

Poor Paul was always kind of suspicious of people, maybe on account of how Jim had kept foolin' him. Paul wouldn't have much to do with anybody only his own mother and Doc Stair and a girl here in town named Julie Gregg. That is, she ain't a girl no more, but pretty near thirty or over.

When Doc first come to town, Paul seemed to feel like here was a real friend and he hung around Doc's office most of the w'ile; the only time he wasn't there was when he'd go home to eat or sleep or when he seen Julie Gregg doin' her shoppin'.

When he looked out Doc's window and seen her, he'd run downstairs and join her and tag along with her to the different stores. The poor boy was crazy about Julie and she always treated him mighty nice and made him feel like he was welcome, though of course it wasn't nothin' but pity on her side.

Doc done all he could to improve Paul's mind and he told me once that he really thought the boy was gettin' better, that they was times when he was as bright and sensible as anybody else.

But I was goin' to tell you about Julie Gregg. Old Man Gregg was in the lumber business, but got to drinkin' and lost the most of his money and when he died, he didn't leave nothin' but the house and just enough insurance for the girl to skimp along on.

Her mother was a kind of a half invalid and didn't hardly ever leave the house. Julie wanted to sell the place and move somewheres else after the old man died, but the mother said she was born here and would die here. It was tough on Julie, as the young people round this town—well, she's too good for them.

She's been away to school and Chicago and New York and different places and they ain't no subject she can't talk on, where you take the rest of the young folks here and you mention anything to them outside of Gloria Swanson or Tommy Meighan and they think you're delirious. Did you see Gloria in Wages of Virtue? You missed somethin'!

Well, Doc Stair hadn't been here more than a week when he come in one day to get shaved and I recognized who he was as he had been pointed out to me, so I told him about my old lady. She's been ailin' for a couple of years and either Doc Gamble or Doc Foote, neither one, seemed to be helpin' her. So he said he would come out and see her, but if she was able to get out herself, it would be better to bring her to his office where he could make a completer examination.

So I took her to his office and w'ile I was waitin' for her in the reception room, in come Julie Gregg. When somebody comes in Doc Stair's office, they's a bell that rings in his inside office so as he can tell they's somebody to see him.

So he left my old lady inside and come out to the front office and that's the first time him and Julie met and I guess it was what they call love at first sight. But it wasn't fifty-fifty. This young fella was the slickest lookin' fella she'd ever seen in this town and she went wild over him. To him she was just a young lady that wanted to see the doctor.

She'd came on about the same business I had. Her mother had been doctorin' for years with Doc Gamble and Doc Foote and without no results. So she'd heard they was a new doc in town and decided to give him a try. He promised to call and see her mother that same day.

I said a minute ago that it was love at first sight on her part. I'm not only judgin' by how she acted afterwards but how she looked at him that first day in his office. I ain't no mind reader, but it was wrote all over her face that she was gone.

Now Jim Kendall, besides bein' a jokesmith and a pretty good drinker, well, Jim was quite a lady-killer. I guess he run pretty wild durin' the time he was on the road for them Carterville people, and besides that, he'd had a couple little affairs of the heart right here in town. As I say, his wife could of divorced him, only she couldn't.

But Jim was like the majority of men, and women, too, I guess. He wanted what he couldn't get. He wanted Julie Gregg and worked his head off tryin' to land her. Only he'd of said bean instead of head.

Well, Jim's habits and his jokes didn't appeal to Julie and of course he was a married man, so he didn't have no more chance than, well, than a rabbit. That's an expression of Jim's himself. When somebody didn't have no chance to get elected or somethin', Jim would always say they didn't have no more chance than a rabbit.

He didn't make no bones about how he felt. Right in here, more than once, in front of the whole crowd, he said he was stuck on Julie and anybody that could get her for him was welcome to his house and his wife and kids included. But she wouldn't have nothin' to do with him; wouldn't even speak to him on the street. He finally seen he wasn't gettin' nowheres with his usual line so he decided to try the rough stuff. He went right up to her house one evenin' and when she opened the door he forced his way in and grabbed her. But she broke loose and before he could stop her, she run in the next room and locked the door and phoned to Joe Barnes. Joe's the marshal. Jim could hear who she was phonin' to and he beat it before Joe got there.

Joe was an old friend of Julie's pa. Joe went to Jim the next day and told him what would happen if he ever done it again.

I don't know how the news of this little affair leaked out. Chances is that Joe Barnes told his wife and she told somebody else's wife and they told their husband. Anyways, it did leak out and Hod Meyers had the nerve to kid Jim about it, right here in this shop. Jim didn't deny nothin' and kind of laughed it off and said for us all to wait; that lots of people had tried to make a monkey out of him, but he always got even.

Meanw'ile everybody in town was wise to Julie's bein' wild mad over the Doc. I don't suppose she had any idear how her face changed when him and her was together; of course she couldn't of, or she'd of kept away from him. And she didn't know that we was all noticin' how many times she made excuses to go up to his office or pass it on the other side of the street and look up in his window to see if he was there. I felt sorry for her and so did most other people.

Hod Meyers kept rubbin' it into Jim about how the Doc had cut him out. Jim didn't pay no attention to the kiddin' and you could see he was plannin' one of his jokes.

One trick Jim had was the knack of changin' his voice. He could make you think he was a girl talkin' and he could mimic any man's voice. To show you how good he was along this line, I'll tell you the joke he played on me once.

You know, in most towns of any size, when a man is dead and

needs a shave, why the barber that shaves him soaks him five
dollars for the job; that is, he don't soak *him*, but whoever ordered the shave. I just charge three dollars because personally I
don't mind much shavin' a dead person. They lay a whole lot
stiller than live customers. The only thing is that you don't
feel like talkin' to them and you get kind of lonesome.

Well, about the coldest day we ever had here, two years ago
last winter, the phone rung at the house w'ile I was home to dinner and I answered the phone and it was a woman's voice and
she said she was Mrs. John Scott and her husband was dead and
would I come out and shave him.

Old John had always been a good customer of mine. But
they live seven miles out in the country, on the Streeter road.
Still I didn't see how I could say no.

So I said I would be there, but would have to come in a jitney
and it might cost three or four dollars besides the price of the
shave. So she, or the voice, it said that was all right, so I got
Frank Abbott to drive me out to the place and when I got there,
who should open the door but old John himself! He wasn't no
more dead than, well, than a rabbit.

It didn't take no private detective to figure out who had
played me this little joke. Nobody could of thought it up but
Jim Kendall. He certainly was a card!

I tell you this incident just to show you how he could dis-
guise his voice and make you believe it was somebody else
talkin'. I'd of swore it was Mrs. Scott had called me. Anyways,
some woman.

Well, Jim waited till he had Doc Stair's voice down pat; then
he went after revenge.

He called Julie up on a night when he knew Doc was over
in Carterville. She never questioned but what it was Doc's voice.
Jim said he must see her that night; he couldn't wait no longer
to tell her somethin'. She was all excited and told him to come to
the house. But he said he was expectin' an important long dis-

tance call and wouldn't she please forget her manners for once and come to his office. He said they couldn't nothin' hurt her and nobody would see her and he just *must* talk to her a little w'ile. Well, poor Julie fell for it.

Doc always keeps a night light in his office, so it looked to Julie like they was somebody there.

Meanw'ile Jim Kendall had went to Wright's poolroom, where they was a whole gang amusin' themselves. The most of them had drank plenty of gin, and they was a rough bunch even when sober. They was always strong for Jim's jokes and when he told them to come with him and see some fun they give up their card games and pool games and followed along.

Doc's office is on the second floor. Right outside his door they's a flight of stairs leadin' to the floor above. Jim and his gang hid in the dark behind these stairs.

Well, Julie come up to Doc's door and rung the bell and they was nothin' doin'. She rung it again and rung it seven or eight times. Then she tried the door and found it locked. Then Jim made some kind of a noise and she heard it and waited a minute, and then she says, "Is that you, Ralph?" Ralph is Doc's first name.

They was no answer and it must of came to her all of a sudden that she'd been bunked. She pretty near fell downstairs and the whole gang after her. They chased her all the way home, hollerin', "Is that you, Ralph?" and "Oh, Ralphie, dear, is that you?" Jim says he couldn't holler it himself, as he was laughin' too hard.

Poor Julie! She didn't show up here on Main Street for a long, long time afterward.

And of course Jim and his gang told everybody in town, everybody but Doc Stair. They was scared to tell him, and he might of never knowed only for Paul Dickson. The poor cuckoo, as Jim called him, he was here in the shop one night when Jim was still gloatin' yet over what he'd done to Julie. And Paul took in as much of it as he could understand and he run to Doc with the story.

It's a cinch Doc went up in the air and swore he'd make Jim
suffer. But it was a kind of a delicate thing, because if it got out
that he had beat Jim up, Julie was bound to hear of it and then
she'd know that Doc knew and of course knowin' that he knew
would make it worse for her than ever. He was goin' to do somethin', but it took a lot of figurin'.

Well, it was a couple days later when Jim was here in the shop
again, and so was the cuckoo. Jim was goin' duck-shootin' the
next day and had came in lookin' for Hod Meyers to go with
him. I happened to know that Hod had went over to Carterville
and wouldn't be home till the end of the week. So Jim said he
hated to go alone and he guessed he would call it off. Then poor
Paul spoke up and said if Jim would take him he would go along.
Jim thought a w'ile and then he said, well, he guessed a half-wit
was better than nothin'.

I suppose he was plottin' to get Paul out in the boat and play
some joke on him, like pushin' him in the water. Anyways, he
said Paul could go. He asked him had he ever shot a duck and
Paul said no, he'd never even had a gun in his hands. So Jim said
he could set in the boat and watch him and if he behaved himself, he might lend him his gun for a couple of shots. They made
a date to meet in the mornin' and that's the last I seen of Jim
alive.

Next mornin', I hadn't been open more than ten minutes when
Doc Stair come in. He looked kind of nervous. He asked me
had I seen Paul Dickson. I said no, but I knew where he was, out
duck-shootin' with Jim Kendall. So Doc says that's what he had
heard, and he couldn't understand it because Paul had told him
he wouldn't never have no more to do with Jim as long as he
lived.

He said Paul had told him about the joke Jim had played on
Julie. He said Paul had asked him what he thought of the joke
and the Doc had told him that anybody that would do a thing
like that ought not to be let live.

I said it had been a kind of a raw thing, but Jim just couldn't resist no kind of a joke, no matter how raw. I said I thought he was all right at heart, but just bubblin' over with mischief. Doc turned and walked out.

At noon he got a phone call from old John Scott. The lake where Jim and Paul had went shootin' is on John's place. Paul had come runnin' up to the house a few minutes before and said they'd been an accident. Jim had shot a few ducks and then give the gun to Paul and told him to try his luck. Paul hadn't never handled a gun and he was nervous. He was shakin' so hard that he couldn't control the gun. He let fire and Jim sunk back in the boat, dead.

Doc Stair, bein' the coroner, jumped in Frank Abbott's flivver and rushed out to Scott's farm. Paul and old John was down on the shore of the lake. Paul had rowed the boat to shore, but they'd left the body in it, waitin' for Doc to come.

Doc examined the body and said they might as well fetch it back to town. They was no use leavin' it there or callin' a jury, as it was a plain case of accidental shootin'.

Personally I wouldn't never leave a person shoot a gun in the same boat I was in unless I was sure they knew somethin' about guns. Jim was a sucker to leave a new beginner have his gun, let alone a half-wit. It probably served Jim right, what he got. But still we miss him round here. He certainly was a card!

Comb it wet or dry?

I CAN'T BREATHE

I am staying here at the Inn for two weeks with my Uncle Nat and Aunt Jule and I think I will keep a kind of diary while I am here to help pass the time and so I can have a record of things that happen though goodness knows there isn't lightly to anything happen, that is anything exciting with Uncle Nat and Aunt Jule making the plans as they are both at least 35 years old and maybe older.

Dad and mother are abroad to be gone a month and me coming here is supposed to be a recompence for them not taking me with them. A fine recompence to be left with old people that come to a place like this to rest. Still it would be a heavenly place under different conditions, for instance if Walter were here, too. It would be heavenly if he were here, the very thought of it makes my heart stop.

I can't stand it. I won't think about it.

This is our first separation since we have been engaged, nearly 17 days. It will be 17 days tomorrow. And the hotel orchestra at dinner this evening played that old thing "Oh how I miss you tonight" and it seemed as if they must be playing it for my benefit though of course the person in that song is talking about how they miss their mother though of course I miss mother too, but a person gets used to missing their mother and it isn't like Walter or the person you are engaged to.

But there won't be any more separations much longer, we are going to be married in December even if mother does laugh when I talk to her about it because she says I am crazy to even think of getting married at 18.

She got married herself when she was 18, but of course that was "different," she wasn't crazy like I am, she knew whom she was marrying. As if Walter were a policeman or a foreigner or something. And she says she was only engaged once while I have been engaged at least five times a year since I was 14, of course it really isn't as bad as that and I have really only been really what I call engaged six times altogether, but is getting engaged my fault when they keep insisting and hammering at you and if you didn't say yes they would never go home.

But it is different with Walter. I honestly believe if he had not asked me I would have asked him. Of course I wouldn't have, but I would have died. And this is the first time I have ever been engaged to be really married. The other times when they talked about when we should get married I just laughed at them, but I hadn't been engaged to Walter ten minutes when he brought up the subject of marriage and I didn't laugh. I wouldn't be engaged to him unless it was to be married. I couldn't stand it.

Anyway mother may as well get used to the idea because it is "No Foolin'" this time and we have got our plans all made and I am going to be married at home and go out to California and Hollywood on our honeymoon. December, five months away. I can't stand it. I can't wait.

There were a couple of awfully nice looking boys sitting together alone in the dining-room tonight. One of them wasn't so much, but the other was cute. And he——

There's the dance orchestra playing "Always," what they played at the Biltmore the day I met Walter. "Not for just an hour not for just a day." I can't live. I can't breathe.

July 13

This has been a much more exciting day than I expected under the circumstances. In the first place I got two long night letters, one from Walter and one from Gordon Flint. I don't see how Walter ever had the nerve to send his, there was everything in it and it must have been horribly embarrassing for him while the telegraph operator was reading it over and counting the words to say nothing of embarrassing the operator.

But the one from Gordon was a kind of a shock. He just got back from a trip around the world, left last December to go on it and got back yesterday and called up our house and Helga gave him my address, and his telegram, well it was nearly as bad as Walter's. The trouble is that Gordon and I were engaged when he went away, or at least he thought so and he wrote to me right along all the time he was away and sent cables and things and for a while I answered his letters, but then I lost track of his itinery and couldn't write to him any more and when I got really engaged to Walter I couldn't let Gordon know because I had no idea where he was besides not wanting to spoil his trip.

And now he still thinks we are engaged and he is going to call me up tomorrow from Chicago and how in the world can I explain things and get him to understand because he is really serious and I like him ever and ever so much and in lots of ways he is nicer than Walter, not really nicer but better looking and there is no comparison between their dancing. Walter simply can't learn to dance, that is really dance. He says it is because he is flat footed, he says that as a joke, but it is true and I wish to heavens it wasn't.

All forenoon I thought and thought and thought about what to say to Gordon when he calls up and finally I couldn't stand thinking about it any more and just made up my mind I wouldn't think about it any more. But I will tell the truth though it will kill me to hurt him.

I went down to lunch with Uncle Nat and Aunt Jule and they were going out to play golf this afternoon and were insisting that I go with them, but I told them I had a headache and then I had a terrible time getting them to go without me. I didn't have a headache at all and just wanted to be alone to think about Walter and besides when you play with Uncle Nat he is always correcting your stance or your swing or something and always puts his hands on my arms or shoulders to show me the right way and I can't stand it to have old men touch me, even if they are your uncle.

I finally got rid of them and I was sitting watching the tennis when that boy that I saw last night, the cute one, came and sat right next to me and of course I didn't look at him and I was going to smoke a cigarette and found I had left my lighter upstairs and I started to get up and go after it when all of a sudden he was offering me his lighter and I couldn't very well refuse it without being rude. So we got to talking and he is even cuter than he looks, the most original and wittiest person I believe I ever met and I haven't laughed so much in I don't know how long.

For one thing he asked me if I had heard Rockefeller's song and I said no and he began singing "Oil alone." Then he asked me if I knew the orange juice song and I told him no again and he said it was "Orange juice sorry you made me cry." I was in hysterics before we had been together ten minutes.

His name is Frank Caswell and he has been out of Dartmouth a year and is 24 years old. That isn't so terribly old, only two years older than Walter and three years older than Gordon. I hate the name Frank, but Caswell is all right and he is so cute.

He was out in California last winter and visited Hollywood and met everybody in the world and it is fascinating to listen to him. He met Norma Shearer and he said he thought she was the prettiest thing he had ever seen. What he said was "I did think she was the prettiest girl in the world, till today." I was going to pretend I didn't get it, but I finally told him to be sensible or I would never be able to believe anything he said.

Well, he wanted me to dance with him tonight after dinner and the next question was how to explain how we had met each other to Uncle Nat and Aunt Jule. Frank said he would fix that all right and sure enough he got himself introduced to Uncle Nat when Uncle Nat came in from golf and after dinner Uncle Nat introduced him to me and Aunt Jule too and we danced together all evening, that is not Aunt Jule. They went to bed, thank heavens.

He is a heavenly dancer, as good as Gordon. One dance we were dancing and for one of the encores the orchestra played "In a cottage small by a waterfall" and I simply couldn't dance to it. I just stopped still and said "Listen, I can't bear it, I can't breathe" and poor Frank thought I was sick or something and I had to explain that that was the tune the orchestra played the night I sat at the next table to Jack Barrymore at Barney Gallant's.

I made him sit out that encore and wouldn't let him talk till they got through playing it. Then they played something else and I was all right again and Frank told me about meeting Jack Barrymore. Imagine meeting him. I couldn't live.

I promised Aunt Jule I would go to bed at eleven and it is way past that now, but I am all ready for bed and have just been writing this. Tomorrow Gordon is going to call up and what will I say to him? I just won't think about it.

July 14

Gordon called up this morning from Chicago and it was wonderful to hear his voice again though the connection was terrible. He asked me if I still loved him and I tried to tell him no, but I knew that would mean an explanation and the connection was so bad that I never could make him understand so I said yes, but I almost whispered it purposely, thinking he wouldn't hear me, but he heard me all right and he said that made everything all right with the world. He said he thought I had stopped loving him because I had stopped writing.

I wish the connection had been decent and I could have told him how things were, but now it is terrible because he is planning to get to New York the day I get there and heaven knows what I will do because Walter will be there, too. I just won't think about it.

Aunt Jule came in my room just after I was through talking to Gordon, thank heavens. The room was full of flowers. Walter had sent me some and so had Frank. I got another long night letter from Walter, just as silly as the first one. I wish he would say those things in letters instead of night letters so everybody in the world wouldn't see them. Aunt Jule wanted me to read it aloud to her. I would have died.

While she was still in the room, Frank called up and asked me to play golf with him and I said all right and Aunt Jule said she was glad my headache was gone. She was trying to be funny.

I played golf with Frank this afternoon. He is a beautiful golfer and it is thrilling to watch him drive, his swing is so much more graceful than Walter's. I asked him to watch me swing and tell me what was the matter with me, but he said he couldn't look at anything but my face and there wasn't anything the matter with that.

He told me the boy who was here with him had been called home and he was glad of it because I might have liked him, the other boy, better than himself. I told him that couldn't be possible and he asked me if I really meant that and I said of course, but I smiled when I said it so he wouldn't take it too seriously.

We danced again tonight and Uncle Nat and Aunt Jule sat

with us a while and danced a couple of dances themselves, but they were really there to get better acquainted with Frank and see if he was all right for me to be with. I know they certainly couldn't have enjoyed their own dancing, no old people really can enjoy it because they can't really *do* anything.

They were favorably impressed with Frank I think, at least Aunt Jule didn't say I must be in bed at eleven, but just not to stay up too late. I guess it is a big surprise to a girl's parents and aunts and uncles to find out that the boys you go around with are all right, they always seem to think that if I seem to like somebody and the person pays a little attention to me, why he must be a convict or a policeman or a drunkard or something queer.

Frank had some more songs for me tonight. He asked me if I knew the asthma song and I said I didn't and he said "Oh, you must know that. It goes yes, sir, asthma baby." Then he told me about the underwear song, "I underwear my baby is tonight." He keeps you in hysterics and yet he has his serious side, in fact he was awfully serious when he said good night to me and his eyes simply shown. I wish Walter were more like him in some ways, but I mustn't think about that.

July 15

I simply can't live and I know I'll never sleep tonight. I am in a terrible predicament or rather I won't know whether I really am or not till tomorrow and that is what makes it so terrible.

After we had danced two or three dances, Frank asked me to go for a ride with him and we went for a ride in his car and he had had some cocktails and during the ride he had some drinks out of a flask and finally he told me he loved me and I said not to be silly, but he said he was perfectly serious and he certainly acted that way. He asked me if I loved anybody else and I said yes and he asked if I didn't love him more than anybody else and I said yes, but only because I thought he had probably had too much to drink and wouldn't remember it anyway and the best thing to do was humor him under the circumstances.

Then all of a sudden he asked me when I could marry him and I said, just as a joke, that I couldn't possibly marry him before December. He said that was a long time to wait, but I was certainly worth waiting for and he said a lot of other things and maybe I humored him a little too much, but that is just the trouble, I don't know.

I was absolutely sure he was tight and would forget the whole thing, but that was early in the evening, and when we said good night he was a whole lot more sober than he had been and now I am not sure how it stands. If he doesn't remember anything about it, of course I am all right. But if he does remember and if he took me seriously, I will simply have to tell him about Walter and maybe about Gordon, too. And it isn't going to be easy. The suspense is what is maddening and I know I'll never live through this night.

July 16

I can't stand it, I can't breathe, life is impossible. Frank remembered everything about last night and firmly believes we are engaged and going to be married in December. His people live in New York and he says he is going back when I do and have them meet me.

Of course it can't go on and tomorrow I will tell him about Walter or Gordon or both of them. I know it is going to hurt him terribly, perhaps spoil his life and I would give anything in the world not to have had it happen. I hate so to hurt him because he is so nice besides being so cute and attractive.

He sent me the loveliest flowers this morning and called up at ten and wanted to know how soon he could see me and I hope the girl wasn't listening in because the things he said were, well, like Walter's night letters.

And that is another terrible thing, today I didn't get a night letter from Walter, but there was a regular letter instead and I carried it around in my purse all this afternoon and evening and never remembered to read it till ten minutes ago when I came up in the room. Walter is worried because I have only sent him two telegrams and written him one letter since I have been here, he would be a lot more worried if he knew what has happened now, though of course it can't make any difference because he is the one I am really engaged to be married to and the one I told mother I was going to marry in December and I wouldn't dare tell her it was somebody else.

I met Frank for lunch and we went for a ride this afternoon and he was so much in love and so lovely to me that I simply did not have the heart to tell him the truth, I am surely going to tell him tomorrow and telling him today would have just meant one more day of unhappiness for both of us.

He said his people had plenty of money and his father had offered to take him into partnership and he might accept, but he thinks his true vocation is journalism with a view to eventually writing novels and if I was willing to undergo a few hardships just at first we would probably both be happier later on if he was doing something he really liked. I didn't know what to say, but finally I said I wanted him to suit himself and money wasn't everything.

He asked me where I would like to go on my honeymoon and I suppose I ought to have told him my honeymoon was all planned, that I was going to California, with Walter, but all I said was that I had always wanted to go to California and he was enthusiastic and said that is where we would surely go and he would take me to Hollywood and introduce me to all those wonderful people he met there last winter. It nearly takes my breath

away to think of it, going there with someone who really knows
people and has the entrée.

We danced again tonight, just two or three dances, and then
went out and sat in the tennis-court, but I came upstairs early
because Aunt Jule had acted kind of funny at dinner. And I
wanted to be alone, too, and think, but the more I think the
worse it gets.

Sometimes I wish I were dead, maybe that is the only solution
and it would be best for everyone concerned. I *will* die if things
keep on the way they have been. But of course tomorrow it will
be all over, with Frank I mean, for I must tell him the truth no
matter how much it hurts us both. Though I don't care how
much it hurts me. The thought of hurting him is what is driving
me mad. I can't bear it.

July 18

I have skipped a day. I was busy every minute of yesterday
and so exhausted when I came upstairs that I was tempted to fall
into bed with all my clothes on. First Gordon called me up from
Chicago to remind me that he would be in New York the day
I got there and that when he comes he wants me all to himself
all the time and we can make plans for our wedding. The connection was bad again and I just couldn't explain to him about Walter.

I had an engagement with Frank for lunch and just as we were
going in another long distance call came, from Walter this time.
He wanted to know why I haven't written more letters and sent
him more telegrams and asked me if I still loved him and of course
I told him yes because I really do. Then he asked if I had met any
men here and I told him I had met one, a friend of Uncle Nat's.
After all it was Uncle Nat who introduced me to Frank. He re-

minded me that he would be in New York on the 25th which is
the day I expect to get home, and said he would have theater
tickets for that night and we would go somewhere afterwards and
dance.

Frank insisted on knowing who had kept me talking so long
and I told him it was a boy I had known a long while, a very dear
friend of mine and a friend of my family's. Frank was jealous
and kept asking questions till I thought I would go mad. He was
so serious and kind of cross and gruff that I gave up the plan of
telling him the truth till some time when he is in better spirits.

I played golf with Frank in the afternoon and we took a ride
last night and I wanted to get in early because I had promised
both Walter and Gordon that I would write them long letters,
but Frank wouldn't bring me back to the Inn till I had named a
definite date in December. I finally told him the 10th and he said
all right if I was sure that wasn't a Sunday. I said I would have to
look it up but as a matter of fact I know the 10th falls on a Friday because the date Walter and I have agreed on for our wedding is Saturday the 11th.

Today has just been the same thing over again, two more night
letters, a long distance call from Chicago, golf and a ride
with Frank, and the room full of flowers. But tomorrow I am
going to tell Frank and I am going to write Gordon a long letter and tell him, too, because this simply can't go on any longer.
I can't breathe. I can't live.

July 21

I wrote to Gordon yesterday, but I didn't say anything about
Walter because I don't think it is a thing a person ought to do
by letter. I can tell him when he gets to New York and then I
will be sure that he doesn't take it too hard and I can promise
him that I will be friends with him always and make him prom-

ise not to do anything silly, while if I told it to him in a letter there is no telling what he would do, there all alone.

And I haven't told Frank because he hasn't been feeling well, he is terribly sunburned and it hurts him terribly so he can hardly play golf or dance, and I want him to be feeling his best when I do tell him, but whether he is all right or not I simply must tell him tomorrow because he is actually planning to leave here on the same train with us Saturday night and I can't let him do that.

Life is so hopeless and it could be so wonderful. For instance how heavenly it would be if I could marry Frank first and stay married to him five years and he would be the one who would take me to Hollywood and maybe we could go on parties with Norman Kerry and Jack Barrymore and Buster Collier and Marion Davies and Lois Moran.

And at the end of five years Frank could go into journalism and write novels and I would only be 23 and I could marry Gordon and he would be ready for another trip around the world and he could show me things better than someone who had never seen them before.

Gordon and I would separate at the end of five years and I would be 28 and I know of lots of women that never even got married the first time till they were 28 though I don't suppose that was their fault, but I would marry Walter then, for after all he is the one I really love and want to spend most of my life with and I wouldn't care whether he could dance or not when I was that old. Before long we would be as old as Uncle Nat and Aunt Jule and I certainly wouldn't want to dance at their age when all you can do is just hobble around the floor. But Walter is so wonderful as a companion and we would enjoy the same things and be pals and maybe we would begin to have children.

But that is all impossible though it wouldn't be if older people just had sense and would look at things the right way.

It is only half past ten, the earliest I have gone to bed in weeks, but I am worn out and Frank went to bed early so he could put cold cream on his sunburn.

Listen, diary, the orchestra is playing "Limehouse Blues." The first tune I danced to with Merle Oliver, two years ago. I can't stand it. And how funny that they should play that old tune tonight of all nights, when I have been thinking of Merle off and on all day, and I hadn't thought of him before in weeks and weeks. I wonder where he is, I wonder if it is just an accident or if it means I am going to see him again. I simply mustn't think about it or I'll die.

July 22

I knew it wasn't an accident. I knew it must mean something, and it did.

Merle is coming here today, here to this Inn, and just to see me. And there can only be one reason. And only one answer. I knew that when I heard his voice calling from Boston. How could I ever had thought I loved anyone else? How could he ever have thought I meant it when I told him I was engaged to George Morse?

A whole year and he still cares and I still care. That shows we were always intended for each other and for no one else. I won't make *him* wait till December. I doubt if we even wait till dad and mother get home. And as for a honeymoon I will go with him to Long Beach or the Bronx Zoo, wherever he wants to take me.

After all this is the best way out of it, the only way. I won't have to say anything to Frank, he will guess when he sees me with Merle. And when I get home Sunday and Walter and Gordon call me up, I will invite them both to dinner and Merle can tell them himself, with two of them there it will only hurt each one half as much as if they were alone.

The train is due at 2:40, almost three hours from now. I can't wait. And what if it should be late? I can't stand it.

ALIBI IKE

His right name was Frank X. Farrell, and I guess the X stood for
"Excuse me." Because he never pulled a play, good or bad, on or
off the field, without apologizin' for it.

"Alibi Ike" was the name Carey wished on him the first day he
reported down South. O' course we all cut out the "Alibi" part
of it right away for the fear he would overhear it and bust
somebody. But we called him "Ike" right to his face and the rest
of it was understood by everybody on the club except Ike himself.

He ast me one time, he says:

"What do you all call me Ike for? I ain't no Yid."

"Carey give you the name," I says. "It's his nickname for
everybody he takes a likin' to."

"He mustn't have only a few friends then," says Ike. "I never
heard him say 'Ike' to nobody else."

But I was goin' to tell you about Carey namin' him. We'd
been workin' out two weeks and the pitchers was showin' somethin' when this bird joined us. His first day out he stood up there
so good and took such a reef at the old pill that he had everyone
lookin'. Then him and Carey was together in left field, catchin'
fungoes, and it was after we was through for the day that Carey
told me about him.

"What do you think of Alibi Ike?" ast Carey.

"Who's that?" I says.

"This here Farrell in the outfield," says Carey.

"He looks like he could hit," I says.

"Yes," says Carey, "but he can't hit near as good as he can apologize."

Then Carey went on to tell me what Ike had been pullin' out there. He'd dropped the first fly ball that was hit to him and told Carey his glove wasn't broke in good yet, and Carey says the glove could easy of been Kid Gleason's gran'father. He made a whale of a catch out o' the next one and Carey says "Nice work!" or somethin' like that, but Ike says he could of caught the ball with his back turned only he slipped when he started after it and, besides that, the air currents fooled him.

"I thought you done well to get to the ball," says Carey.

"I ought to been settin' under it," says Ike.

"What did you hit last year?" Carey ast him.

"I had malaria most o' the season," says Ike. "I wound up with .356.

"Where would I have to go to get malaria?" says Carey, but Ike didn't wise up.

I and Carey and him set at the same table together for supper. It took him half an hour longer'n us to eat because he had to excuse himself every time he lifted his fork.

"Doctor told me I needed starch," he'd say, and then toss a shoveful o' potatoes into him. Or, "They ain't much meat on one o' these chops," he'd tell us, and grab another one. Or he'd say: "Nothin' like onions for a cold," and then he'd dip into the perfumery.

"Better try that apple sauce," says Carey. "It'll help your malaria."

"Whose malaria?" says Ike. He'd forgot already why he didn't only hit .356 last year.

I and Carey begin to lead him on.

"Whereabouts did you say your home was?" I ast him.

"I live with my folks," he says. "We live in Kansas City—not right down in the business part—outside a ways."

"How's that come?" says Carey. "I should think you'd get rooms in the post office."

But Ike was too busy curin' his cold to get that one.

"Are you married?" I ast him.

"No," he says. "I never run round much with girls, except to shows onct in a wile and parties and dances and roller skatin'."

"Never take 'em to the prize fights, eh?" says Carey.

"We don't have no real good bouts," says Ike. "Just bush stuff. And I never figured a boxin' match was a place for the ladies."

Well, after supper he pulled a cigar out and lit it. I was just goin' to ask him what he done it for, but he beat me to it.

"Kind o' rests a man to smoke after a good work-out," he says. "Kind o' settles a man's supper, too."

"Looks like a pretty good cigar," says Carey.

"Yes," says Ike. "A friend o' mine give it to me—a fella in Kansas City that runs a billiard room."

"Do you play billiards?" I ast him.

"I used to play a fair game," he says. "I'm all out o' practice now—can't hardly make a shot."

We coaxed him into a four-handed battle, him and Carey against Jack Mack and I. Say, he couldn't play billiards as good as Willie Hoppe; not quite. But to hear him tell it, he didn't make a good shot all evenin'. I'd leave him an awful-lookin' layout and he'd gather 'em up in one try and then run a couple o' hundred, and between every carom he'd say he'd put too much stuff on the ball, or the English didn't take, or the table wasn't true, or his stick was crooked, or somethin'. And all the time he had the balls actin' like they was Dutch soldiers and him Kaiser William. We started out to play fifty points, but we had to make it a thousand so as I and Jack and Carey could try the table.

The four of us set round the lobby a wile after we was through

playin', and when it got along toward bedtime Carey whispered
to me and says:

"Ike'd like to go to bed, but he can't think up no excuse."

Carey hadn't hardly finished whisperin' when Ike got up and
pulled it:

"Well, good night, boys," he says. "I ain't sleepy, but I got
some gravel in my shoes and it's killin' my feet."

We knowed he hadn't never left the hotel since we'd came in
from the grounds and changed our clo'es. So Carey says:

"I should think they'd take them gravel pits out o' the billiard
room."

But Ike was already on his way to the elevator, limpin'.

"He's got the world beat," says Carey to Jack and I. "I've knew
lots o' guys that had an alibi for every mistake they made; I've
heard pitchers say that the ball slipped when somebody cracked
one off'n 'em; I've heard infielders complain of a sore arm after
heavin' one into the stand, and I've saw outfielders tooken sick
with a dizzy spell when they've misjudged a fly ball. But this
baby can't even go to bed without apologizin', and I bet he
excuses himself to the razor when he gets ready to shave."

"And at that," says Jack, "he's goin' to make us a good man."

"Yes," says Carey, "unless rheumatism keeps his battin' average down to .400."

Well, sir, Ike kept whalin' away at the ball all through the trip
till everybody knowed he'd won a job. Cap had him in there
regular the last few exhibition games and told the newspaper
boys a week before the season opened that he was goin' to start
him in Kane's place.

"You're there, kid," says Carey to Ike, the night Cap made the
'nnouncement. "They ain't many boys that wins a big league
berth their third year out."

"I'd of been up here a year ago," says Ike, "only I was bent
over all season with lumbago."

II

It rained down in Cincinnati one day and somebody organized a little game o' cards. They was shy two men to make six and ast I and Carey to play.

"I'm with you if you get Ike and make it seven-handed," says Carey.

So they got a hold of Ike and we went up to Smitty's room.

"I pretty near forgot how many you deal," says Ike. "It's been a long wile since I played."

I and Carey give each other the wink, and sure enough, he was just as ig'orant about poker as billiards. About the second hand, the pot was opened two or three ahead of him, and they was three in when it come his turn. It cost a buck, and he throwed in two.

"It's raised, boys," somebody says.

"Gosh, that's right, I did raise it," says Ike.

"Take out a buck if you didn't mean to tilt her," says Carey.

"No," says Ike, "I'll leave it go."

Well, it was raised back at him and then he made another mistake and raised again. They was only three left in when the draw come. Smitty'd opened with a pair o' kings and he didn't help 'em. Ike stood pat. The guy that'd raised him back was flushin' and he didn't fill. So Smitty checked and Ike bet and didn't get no call. He tossed his hand away, but I grabbed it and give it a look. He had king, queen, jack and two tens. Alibi Ike he must have seen me peekin', for he leaned over and whispered to me.

"I overlooked my hand," he says. "I thought all the wile it was a straight."

"Yes," I says, "that's why you raised twice by mistake."

They was another pot that he come into with tens and fours.

It was tilted a couple o' times and two o' the strong fellas drawed ahead of Ike. They each drawed one. So Ike throwed away his little pair and come out with four tens. And they was four treys against him. Carey'd looked at Ike's discards and then he says:

"This lucky bum busted two pair."

"No, no, I didn't," says Ike.

"Yes, yes, you did," says Carey, and showed us the two fours.

"What do you know about that?" says Ike. "I'd of swore one was a five spot."

Well, we hadn't had no pay day yet, and after a wile everybody except Ike was goin' shy. I could see him getting restless and I was wonderin' how he'd make the get-away. He tried two or three times. "I got to buy some collars before supper," he says.

"No hurry," says Smitty. "The stores here keeps open all night in April."

After a minute he opened up again.

"My uncle out in Nebraska ain't expected to live," he says. "I ought to send a telegram."

"Would that save him?" says Carey.

"No, it sure wouldn't," says Ike, "but I ought to leave my old man know where I'm at."

"When did you hear about your uncle?" says Carey.

"Just this mornin'," says Ike.

"Who told you?" ast Carey.

"I got a wire from my old man," says Ike.

"Well," says Carey, "your old man knows you're still here yet this afternoon if you was here this mornin'. Trains leavin' Cincinnati in the middle o' the day don't carry no ball clubs."

"Yes," says Ike, "that's true. But he don't know where I'm goin' to be next week."

"Ain't he got no schedule?" ast Carey.

"I sent him one openin' day," says Ike, "but it takes mail a long time to get to Idaho."

"I thought your old man lived in Kansas City," says Carey.

"He does when he's home," says Ike.

"But now," says Carey, "I s'pose he's went to Idaho so as he can be near your sick uncle in Nebraska."

"He's visitin' my other uncle in Idaho."

"Then how does he keep posted about your sick uncle?" ast Carey.

"He don't," says Ike. "He don't even know my other uncle's sick. That's why I ought to wire and tell him."

"Good night!" says Carey.

"What town in Idaho is your old man at?" I says.

Ike thought it over.

"No town at all," he says. "But he's near a town."

"Near what town?" I says.

"Yuma," says Ike.

Well, by this time he'd lost two or three pots and he was desperate. We was playin' just as fast as we could, because we seen we couldn't hold him much longer. But he was tryin' so hard to frame an escape that he couldn't pay no attention to the cards, and it looked like we'd get his whole pile away from him if we could make him stick.

The telephone saved him. The minute it begun to ring, five of us jumped for it. But Ike was there first.

"Yes," he says, answerin' it. "This is him. I'll come right down."

And he slammed up the receiver and beat it out o' the door without even sayin' good-by.

"Smitty'd ought to locked the door," says Carey.

"What did he win?" ast Carey.

We figured it up—sixty-odd bucks.

"And the next time we ask him to play," says Carey, "his fingers will be so stiff he can't hold the cards."

Well, we set round a wile talkin' it over, and pretty soon the telephone rung again. Smitty answered it. It was a friend of his'n from Hamilton and he wanted to know why Smitty didn't hurry down. He was the one that had called before and Ike had told him he was Smitty.

"Ike'd ought to split with Smitty's friend," says Carey.

"No," I says, "he'll need all he won. It costs money to buy collars and to send telegrams from Cincinnati to your old man in Texas and keep him posted on the health o' your uncle in Cedar Rapids, D.C."

III

And you ought to heard him out there on that field! They wasn't a day when he didn't pull six or seven, and it didn't make no difference whether he was goin' good or bad. If he popped up in the pinch he should of made a base hit and the reason he didn't was so-and-so. And if he cracked one for three bases he ought to had a home run, only the ball wasn't lively, or the wind brought it back, or he tripped on a lump o' dirt, roundin' first base.

They was one afternoon in New York when he beat all records. Big Marquard was workin' against us and he was good.

In the first innin' Ike hit one clear over that right field stand, but it was a few feet foul. Then he got another foul and then the count come to two and two. Then Rube slipped one acrost on him and he was called out.

"What do you know about that!" he says afterward on the bench. "I lost count. I thought it was three and one, and I took a strike."

"You took a strike all right," says Carey. "Even the umps knowed it was a strike."

"Yes," says Ike, "but you can bet I wouldn't of took it if I'd knew it was the third one. The score board had it wrong."

"That score board ain't for you to look at," says Cap. "It's for you to hit that old pill against."

"Well," says Ike, "I could of hit that one over the score board if I'd knew it was the third."

"Was it a good ball?" I says.

"Well, no, it wasn't," says Ike. "It was inside."

"How far inside?" says Carey.

"Oh, two or three inches or half a foot," says Ike.

"I guess you wouldn't of threatened the score board with it then," says Cap.

"I'd of pulled it down the right foul line if I hadn't thought he'd call it a ball," says Ike.

Well, in New York's part o' the innin' Doyle cracked one and Ike run back a mile and a half and caught it with one hand. We was all sayin' what a whale of a play it was, but he had to apologize just the same as for gettin' struck out.

"That stand's so high," he says, "that a man don't never see a ball till it's right on top o' you."

"Didn't you see that one?" ast Cap.

"Not at first," says Ike; "not till it raised up above the roof o' the stand."

"Then why did you start back as soon as the ball was hit?" says Cap.

"I knowed by the sound that he'd got a good hold of it," says Ike.

"Yes," says Cap, "but how'd you know what direction to run in?"

"Doyle usually hits 'em that way, the way I run," says Ike.

"Why don't you play blindfolded?" says Carey.

"Might as well, with that big high stand to bother a man," says Ike. "If I could of saw the ball all the time I'd of got it in my hip pocket."

Along in the fifth we was one run to the bad and Ike got on with one out. On the first ball throwed to Smitty, Ike went down. The ball was outside and Meyers throwed Ike out by ten feet.

You could see Ike's lips movin' all the way to the bench and when he got there he had his piece learned.

"Why didn't he swing?" he says.

"Why didn't you wait for his sign?" says Cap.

"He give me his sign," says Ike.

"What is his sign with you?" says Cap.

"Pickin' up some dirt with his right hand," says Ike.

"Well, I didn't see him do it," Cap says.

"He done it all right," says Ike.

Well, Smitty went out and they wasn't no more argument till they come in for the next innin'. Then Cap opened it up.

"You fellas better get your signs straight," he says.

"Do you mean me?" says Smitty.

"Yes," Cap says. "What's your sign with Ike?"

"Slidin' my left hand up to the end of the bat and back," says Smitty.

"Do you hear that, Ike?" ast Cap.

"What of it?" says Ike.

"You says his sign was pickin' up dirt and he says it's slidin' his hand. Which is right?"

"I'm right," says Smitty. "But if you're arguin' about him goin' last innin', I didn't give him no sign."

"You pulled your cap down with your right hand, didn't you?" ast Ike.

"Well, s'pose I did," says Smitty. "That don't mean nothin'. I never told you to take that for a sign, did I?"

"I thought maybe you meant to tell me and forgot," says Ike.

They couldn't none of us answer that and they wouldn't of been no more said if Ike had of shut up. But wile we was settin' there Carey got on with two out and stole second clean.

"There!" says Ike. "That's what I was tryin' to do and I'd of got away with it if Smitty'd swang and bothered the Indian."

"Oh," says Smitty. "You was tryin' to steal then, was you? I thought you claimed I give you the hit and run."

"I didn't claim no such thing," says Ike. "I thought maybe you might of gave me a sign, but I was goin' anyway because I thought I had a good start."

Cap prob'ly would of hit him with a bat, only just about that time Doyle booted one on Hayes and Carey come acrost with the run that tied.

Well, we go into the ninth finally, one and one, and Marquard walks McDonald with nobody out.

"Lay it down," says Cap to Ike.

And Ike goes up there with orders to bunt and cracks the first ball into that right-field stand! It was fair this time, and we're two ahead, but I didn't think about that at the time. I was too busy watchin' Cap's face. First he turned pale and then he got red as fire and then he got blue and purple, and finally he just laid back and busted out laughin'. So we wasn't afraid to laugh ourselfs when we seen him doin' it, and when Ike come in everybody on the bench was in hysterics.

But instead o' takin' advantage, Ike had to try and excuse himself. His play was to shut up and he didn't know how to make it.

"Well," he says, "if I hadn't hit quite so quick at that one I bet it'd of cleared the center-field fence."

Cap stopped laughin'.

"It'll cost you plain fifty," he says.

"What for?" says Ike.

"When I say 'bunt' I mean 'bunt,'" says Cap.

"You didn't say 'bunt,'" says Ike.

"I says 'Lay it down,'" says Cap. "If that don't mean 'bunt,' what does it mean?"

"'Lay it down' means 'bunt' all right," says Ike, "but I understood you to say 'Lay on it.'"

"All right," says Cap, "and the little misunderstandin' will cost you fifty."

Ike didn't say nothin' for a few minutes. Then he had another bright idear.

"I was just kiddin' about misunderstandin' you," he says. "I knowed you wanted me to bunt."

"Well, then, why didn't you bunt?" ast Cap.

"I was goin' to on the next ball," says Ike. "But I thought if I took a good wallop I'd have 'em all fooled. So I walloped at the first one to fool 'em, and I didn't have no intention o' hittin' it."

"You tried to miss it, did you?" says Cap.

"Yes," says Ike.

"How'd you happen to hit it?" ast Cap.

"Well," Ike says, "I was lookin' for him to throw me a fast one and I was goin' to swing under it. But he come with a hook and I met it right square where I was swingin' to go under the fast one."

"Great!" says Cap. "Boys," he says, "Ike's learned how to hit Marquard's curve. Pretend a fast one's comin' and then try to miss it. It's a good thing to know and Ike'd ought to be willin' to pay for the lesson. So I'm goin' to make it a hundred instead o' fifty."

The game wound up 3 to 1. The fine didn't go, because Ike hit like a wild man all through that trip and we made pretty near a clean-up. The night we went to Philly I got him cornered in the car and I says to him:

"Forget them alibis for a wile and tell me somethin'. What'd you do that for, swing that time against Marquard when you was told to bunt?"

"I'll tell you," he says. "That ball he throwed me looked just like the one I struck out on in the first innin' and I wanted to show Cap what I could of done to that other one if I'd knew it was the third strike."

"But," I says, "the one you struck out on in the first innin' was a fast ball."

"So was the one I cracked in the ninth," says Ike.

IV

You've saw Cap's wife, o' course. Well, her sister's about twict as good-lookin' as her, and that's goin' some.

Cap took his missus down to St. Louis the second trip and the other one come down from St. Joe to visit her. Her name is Dolly, and some doll is right.

Well, Cap was goin' to take the two sisters to a show and he wanted a beau for Dolly. He left it to her and she picked Ike. He'd hit three on the nose that afternoon—off'n Sallee, too.

They fell for each other that first evenin. Cap told us how it come off. She begin flatterin' Ike for the star game he'd played and o' course he begin excusin' himself for not doin' better. So she thought he was modest and it went strong with her. And she believed everything he said and that made her solid with him— that and her make-up. They was together every mornin' and evenin' for the five days we was there. In the afternoons Ike played the grandest ball you ever see, hittin' and runnin' the bases like a fool and catchin' everything that stayed in the park.

I told Cap, I says: "You'd ought to keep the doll with us and he'd make Cobb's figures look sick."

But Dolly had to go back to St. Joe and we come home for a long serious.

Well, for the next three weeks Ike had a letter to read every day and he'd set in the clubhouse readin' it till mornin' practice was half over. Cap didn't say nothin' to him, because he was goin' so good. But I and Carey wasted a lot of our time tryin' to get him to own up who the letters was from. Fine chanct!

"What are you readin'?" Carey'd say. "A bill?"

"No," Ike'd say, "not exactly a bill. It's a letter from a fella I used to go to school with."

"High school or college?" I'd ask him.

"College," he'd say.

"What college?" I'd say.

Then he'd stall a wile and then he'd say:

"I didn't go to the college myself, but my friend went there."

"How did it happen you didn't go?" Carey'd ask him.

"Well," he'd say, "they wasn't no colleges near where I lived."

"Didn't you live in Kansas City?" I'd say to him.

One time he'd say he did and another time he didn't. One time he says he lived in Michigan.

"Where at?" says Carey.

"Near Detroit," he says.

"Well," I says, "Detroit's near Ann Arbor and that's where they got the university."

"Yes," says Ike, "they got it there now, but they didn't have it there then."

"I come pretty near goin' to Syracuse," I says, "only they wasn't no railroads runnin' through there in them days."

"Where'd this friend o' yours go to college?" says Carey.

"I forget now," says Ike.

"Was it Carlisle?" ast Carey.

"No," says Ike, "his folks wasn't very well off."

"That's what barred me from Smith," I says.

"I was goin' to tackle Cornell's," says Carey, "but the doctor told me I'd have hay fever if I didn't stay up North."

"Your friend writes long letters," I says.

"Yes," says Ike; "he's tellin' me about a ball player."

"Where does he play?" ast Carey.

"Down in the Texas League—Fort Wayne," says Ike.

"It looks like a girl's writin'," Carey says.

"A girl wrote it," says Ike. "That's my friend's sister, writin' for him."

"Didn't they teach writin' at this here college where he went?" says Carey.

"Sure," Ike says, "they taught writin', but he got his hand cut off in a railroad wreck."

"How long ago?" I says.

"Right after he got out o' college," says Ike.

"Well," I says, "I should think he'd of learned to write with his left hand by this time."

"It's his left hand that was cut off," says Ike; "and he was left-handed."

"You get a letter every day," says Carey. "They're all the same writin'. Is he tellin' you about a different ball player every time he writes?"

"No," Ike says. "It's the same ball player. He just tells me what he does every day."

"From the size o' the letters, they don't play nothin' but double-headers down there," says Carey.

We figured that Ike spent most of his evenin's answerin' the letters from his "friend's sister," so we kept tryin' to date him up for shows and parties to see how he'd duck out of 'em. He was bugs over spaghetti, so we told him one day that they was goin' to be a big feed of it over to Joe's that night and he was invited.

"How long'll it last?" he says.

"Well," we says, "we goin' right over there after the game and stay till they close up."

"I can't go," he says, "unless they leave me come home at eight bells."

"Nothin' doin'," says Carey. "Joe'd get sore."

"I can't go then," says Ike.

"Why not?" I ast him.

"Well," he says, "my landlady locks up the house at eight and I left my key home."

"You can come and stay with me," says Carey.

"No," he says, "I can't sleep in a strange bed."

"How do you get along when we're on the road?" says I.

"I don't never sleep the first night anywheres," he says. "After that I'm all right."

"You'll have time to chase home and get your key right after the game," I told him.

"The key ain't home," says Ike. "I lent it to one o' the other fellas and he's went out o' town and took it with him."

"Couldn't you borry another key off'n the landlady?" Carey ast him.

"No," he says, "that's the only one they is."

Well, the day before we started East again, Ike come into the clubhouse all smiles.

"Your birthday?" I ast him.

"No," he says.

"What do you feel so good about?" I says.

"Got a letter from my old man," he says. "My uncle's goin' to get well."

"Is that the one in Nebraska?" says I.

"Not right in Nebraska," says Ike. "Near there."

But afterwards we got the right dope from Cap. Dolly'd blew in from Missouri and was goin' to make the trip with her sister.

V

Well, I want to alibi Carey and I for what come off in Boston. If we'd of had any idear what we was doin', we'd never did it. They wasn't nobody outside o' maybe Ike and the dame that felt worse over it than I and Carey.

The first two days we didn't see nothin' of Ike and her except out to the park. The rest o' the time they was sight-seein' over to Cambridge and down to Revere and out to Brook-a-line and all the other places where the rubes go.

But when we come into the beanery after the third game Cap's wife called us over.

"If you want to see somethin' pretty," she says, "look at the third finger on Sis's left hand."

Well, o' course we knowed before we looked that it wasn't goin' to be no hangnail. Nobody was su'prised when Dolly blew into the dinin' room with it—a rock that Ike'd bought off'n Diamond Joe the first trip to New York. Only o' course it'd been set into a lady's-size ring instead o' the automobile tire he'd been wearin'.

Cap and his Missus and Ike and Dolly ett supper together, only Ike didn't eat nothin', but just set there blushin' and spillin' things on the table-cloth. I heard him excusin' himself for not havin' no appetite. He says he couldn't never eat when he was clost to the ocean. He'd forgot about them sixty-five oysters he destroyed the first night o' the trip before.

He was goin' to take her to a show, so after supper he went upstairs to change his collar. She had to doll up, too, and o' course Ike was through long before her.

If you remember the hotel in Boston, they's a little parlor where the piano's at and then they's another little parlor openin' off o' that. Well, when Ike come down Smitty was playin' a few chords and I and Carey was harmonizin'. We seen Ike go up to the desk to leave his key and we called him in. He tried to duck away, but we wouldn't stand for it.

We ast him what he was all duded up for and he says he was goin' to the theayter.

"Goin' alone?" says Carey.

"No," he says, "a friend o' mine's goin' with me."

"What do you say if we go along?" says Carey.

"I ain't only got two tickets," he says.

"Well," says Carey, "we can go down there with you and buy our own seats; maybe we can all get together."

"No," says Ike. "They ain't no more seats. They're all sold out."

"We can buy some off'n the scalpers," says Carey.

"I wouldn't if I was you," says Ike. "They say the show's rotten."

"What are you goin' for, then?" I ast.

"I didn't hear about it bein' rotten till I got the tickets," he says.

"Well," I says, "if you don't want to go I'll buy the tickets from you."

"No," says Ike, "I wouldn't want to cheat you. I'm stung and I'll just have to stand for it."

"What are you goin' to do with the girl, leave her here at the hotel?" I says.

"What girl?" says Ike.

"The girl you ett supper with," I says.

"Oh," he says, "we just happened to go into the dinin' room together, that's all. Cap wanted I should set down with 'em."

"I noticed," says Carey, "that she happened to be wearin' that rock you bought off'n Diamond Joe."

"Yes," says Ike. "I lent it to her for a wile."

"Did you lend her the new ring that goes with it?" I says.

"She had that already," says Ike. "She lost the set out of it."

"I wouldn't trust no strange girl with a rock o' mine," says Carey.

"Oh, I guess she's all right," Ike says. "Besides, I was tired o' the stone. When a girl asks you for somethin', what are you goin' to do?"

He started out toward the desk, but we flagged him.

"Wait a minute!" Carey says. "I got a bet with Sam here, and it's up to you to settle it."

"Well," says Ike, "make it snappy. My friend'll be here any minute."

ALIBI IKE   53

"I bet," says Carey, "that you and that girl was engaged to be married."

"Nothin' to it," says Ike.

"Now look here," says Carey, "this is goin' to cost me real money if I lose. Cut out the alibi stuff and give it to us straight Cap's wife just as good as told us you was roped."

Ike blushed like a kid.

"Well, boys," he says, "I may as well own up. You win, Carey."

"Yatta boy!" says Carey. "Congratulations!"

"You got a swell girl, Ike," I says.

"She's a peach," says Smitty.

"Well, I guess she's O. K.," says Ike. "I don't know much about girls."

"Didn't you never run round with 'em?" I says.

"Oh, yes, plenty of 'em," says Ike. "But I never seen none I'd fall for."

"That is, till you seen this one," says Carey.

"Well," says Ike, "this one's O. K., but I wasn't thinkin' about gettin' married yet a wile."

"Who done the askin'—her?" says Carey.

"Oh, no," says Ike, "but sometimes a man don't know what he's gettin' into. Take a good-looking girl, and a man gen'ally almost always does about what she wants him to."

"They couldn't no girl lasso me unless I wanted to be lassoed," says Smitty.

"Oh, I don't know," says Ike. "When a fella gets to feelin' sorry for one of 'em it's all off."

Well, we left him go after shakin' hands all round. But he didn't take Dolly to no show that night. Some time wile we was talkin' she'd came into that other parlor and she'd stood there and heard us. I don't know how much she heard. But it was enough. Dolly and Cap's Missus took the midnight train for New York. And from there Cap's wife sent her on her way back to Missouri.

She'd left the ring and a note for Ike with the clerk. But we didn't ask Ike if the note was from his friend in Fort Wayne, Texas.

VI

When we'd came to Boston Ike was hittin' plain .397. When we got back home he'd fell off to pretty near nothin'. He hadn't drove one out o' the infield in any o' them other Eastern parks, and he didn't even give no excuse for it.

To show you how bad he was, he struck out three times in Brooklyn one day and never opened his trap when Cap ast him what was the matter. Before, if he'd whiffed oncet in a game he'd of wrote a book tellin' why.

Well, we dropped from first place to fifth in four weeks and we was still goin' down. I and Carey was about the only ones in the club that spoke to each other, and all as we did was remind ourself o' what a boner we'd pulled.

"It's goin' to beat us out o' the big money," says Carey.

"Yes," I says. "I don't want to knock my own ball club, but it looks like a one-man team, and when that one man's dauber's down we couldn't trim our whiskers."

"We ought to knew better," says Carey.

"Yes," I says, "but why should a man pull an alibi for bein' engaged to such a bearcat as she was?"

"He shouldn't," says Carey. "But I and you knowed he would or we'd never start talkin' to him about it. He wasn't no more ashamed o' the girl than I am of a regular base hit. But he just can't come clean on no subjec'."

Cap had the whole story, and I and Carey was as pop'lar with him as an umpire.

"What do you want me to do, Cap?" Carey'd say to him before goin' up to hit.

"Use your own judgment," Cap'd tell him. "We want to lose another game."

But finally, one night in Pittsburgh, Cap had a letter from his missus and he come to us with it.

"You fellas," he says, "is the ones that put us on the bum, and if you're sorry I think they's a chancet for you to make good. The old lady's out to St. Joe and she's been tryin' her hardest to fix things up. She's explained that Ike don't mean nothin' with his talk; I've wrote and explained that to Dolly, too. But the old lady says that Dolly says that she can't believe it. But Dolly's still stuck on this baby, and she's pinin' away just the same as Ike. And the old lady says she thinks if you two fellas would write to the girl and explain how you was always kiddin' with Ike and leadin' him on, and how the ball club was all shot to pieces since Ike quit hittin', and how he acted like he was goin' to kill himself, and this and that, she'd fall for it and maybe soften down. Dolly, the old lady says, would believe you before she'd believe I and the old lady, because she thinks it's her we're sorry for, and not him."

Well, I and Carey was only too glad to try and see what we could do. But it wasn't no snap. We wrote about eight letters before we got one that looked good. Then we give it to the stenographer and had it wrote out on a typewriter and both of us signed it.

It was Carey's idear that made the letter good. He stuck in somethin' about the world's serious money that our wives wasn't goin' to spend unless she took pity on a "boy who was so shy and modest that he was afraid to come right out and say that he had asked such a beautiful and handsome girl to become his bride."

That's prob'ly what got her, or maybe she couldn't of held out much longer anyway. It was four days after we sent the letter that Cap heard from his Missus again. We was in Cincinnati.

"We've won," he says to us. "The old lady says that Dolly says she'll give him another chance. But the old lady says it won't do no good for Ike to write a letter. He'll have to go out there."

"Send him to-night," says Carey.

"I'll pay half his fare," I says.

"I'll pay the other half," says Carey.

"No," says Cap, "the club'll pay his expenses. I'll send him scoutin'."

"Are you goin' to send him to-night?"

"Sure," says Cap. "But I'm goin' to break the news to him right now. It's time we win a ball game."

So in the clubhouse, just before the game, Cap told him. And I certainly felt sorry for Rube Benton and Red Ames that afternoon! I and Carey was standin' in front o' the hotel that night when Ike come out with his suitcase.

"Sent home?" I says to him.

"No," he says, "I'm goin' scoutin'."

"Where to?" I says. "Fort Wayne?"

"No, not exactly," he says.

"Well," says Carey, "have a good time."

"I ain't lookin' for no good time," says Ike. "I says I was goin' scoutin'."

"Well, then," says Carey, "I hope you see somebody you like."

"And you better have a drink before you go," I says.

"Well," says Ike, "they claim it helps a cold."

ZONE OF QUIET

"Well," said the Doctor briskly, "how do you feel?"

"Oh, I guess I'm all right," replied the man in bed. "I'm still kind of drowsy, that's all."

"You were under the anesthetic an hour and a half. It's no wonder you aren't wide awake yet. But you'll be better after a good night's rest, and I've left something with Miss Lyons that'll make you sleep. I'm going along now. Miss Lyons will take good care of you."

"I'm off at seven o'clock," said Miss Lyons. "I'm going to a show with my G. F. But Miss Halsey's all right. She's the night floor nurse. Anything you want, she'll get it for you. What can I give him to eat, Doctor?"

"Nothing at all; not till after I've been here tomorrow. He'll be better off without anything. Just see that he's kept quiet. Don't let him talk, and don't talk to him; that is, if you can help it."

"Help it!" said Miss Lyons. "Say, I can be old lady Sphinx herself when I want to! Sometimes I sit for hours—not alone, neither —and never say a word. Just think and think. And dream.

"I had a G. F. in Baltimore, where I took my training; she used to call me Dummy. Not because I'm dumb like some people —you know—but because I'd sit there and not say nothing. She'd say, 'A penny for your thoughts, Eleanor.' That's my first name— Eleanor."

"Well, I must run along. I'll see you in the morning."

"Good-by, Doctor," said the man in bed, as he went out.

"Good-by, Doctor Cox," said Miss Lyons as the door closed.

"He seems like an awful nice fella," said Miss Lyons. "And a good doctor, too. This is the first time I've been on a case with him. He gives a girl credit for having some sense. Most of these doctors treat us like they thought we were Mormons or something. Like Doctor Holland. I was on a case with him last week. He treated me like I was a Mormon or something. Finally, I told him, I said, 'I'm not as dumb as I look.' She died Friday night."

"Who?" asked the man in bed.

"The woman; the case I was on," said Miss Lyons.

"And what did the doctor say when you told him you weren't as dumb as you look?"

"I don't remember," said Miss Lyons. "He said, 'I hope not,' or something. What *could* he say? Gee! It's quarter to seven. I hadn't no idear it was so late. I must get busy and fix you up for the night. And I'll tell Miss Halsey to take good care of you. We're going to see 'What Price Glory?' I'm going with my G. F. Her B. F. gave her the tickets and he's going to meet us after the show and take us to supper.

"Marian—that's my G.F.—she's crazy wild about him. And he's crazy about her, to hear her tell it. But I said to her this noon—she called me up on the phone—I said to her, 'If he's so crazy about you, why don't he propose? He's got plenty of money and no strings tied to him, and as far as I can see there's no reason why he shouldn't marry you if he wants you as bad as you say he does.' So she said maybe he was going to ask her tonight. I told her, 'Don't be silly! Would he drag me along if he was going to ask you?'

"That about him having plenty money, though, that's a joke. He told her he had and she believes him. I haven't met him yet, but he looks in his picture like he's lucky if he's getting twenty-five dollars a week. She thinks he must be rich because he's in Wall Street. I told her, I said, 'That being in Wall Street don't mean nothing. What does he do there? is the question. You know they have to have janitors in those buildings just the same like anywhere else.' But she thinks he's God or somebody.

"She keeps asking me if I don't think he's the best looking thing I ever saw. I tell her yes, sure, but between you and I, I don't believe anybody'd ever mistake him for Richard Barthelmess.

"Oh, say! I saw him the other day, coming out of the Algonquin! He's the best looking thing! Even better looking than on the screen. Roy Stewart."

"What about Roy Stewart?" asked the man in bed.

"Oh, he's the fella I was telling you about," said Miss Lyons. "He's my G. F.'s B. F."

"Maybe I'm a D. F. not to know, but would you tell me what a B. F. and G. F. are?"

"Well, you *are* dumb, aren't you!" said Miss Lyons. "A G. F., that's a girl friend, and a B. F. is a boy friend. I thought everybody knew that.

"I'm going out now and find Miss Halsey and tell her to be nice to you. But maybe I better not."

"Why not?" asked the man in bed.

"Oh, nothing. I was just thinking of something funny that happened last time I was on a case in this hospital. It was the day the man had been operated on and he was the best looking somebody you ever saw. So when I went off duty I told Miss Halsey to be nice to him, like I was going to tell her about you. And when I came back in the morning he was dead. Isn't that funny?"

"Very!"

"Well," said Miss Lyons, "did you have a good night? You look a lot better, anyway. How'd you like Miss Halsey? Did you notice her ankles? She's got pretty near the smallest ankles I ever

saw. Cute. I remember one day Tyler—that's one of the internes
—he said if he could just see our ankles, mine and Miss Halsey's,
he wouldn't know which was which. Of course we don't look
anything alike other ways. She's pretty close to thirty and—
well, nobody'd ever take her for Julia Hoyt. Helen."

"Who's Helen?" asked the man in bed.

"Helen Halsey. Helen; that's her first name. She was engaged to a man in Boston. He was going to Tufts College. He was
going to be a doctor. But he died. She still carries his picture with
her. I tell her she's silly to mope about a man that's been dead
four years. And besides a girl's a fool to marry a doctor. They've
got too many alibis.

"When I marry somebody, he's got to be somebody that has
regular office hours like he's in Wall Street or somewhere. Then
when he don't come home, he'll have to think up something better than being 'on a case.' I used to use that on my sister when we
were living together. When I happened to be out late, I'd tell her
I was on a case. She never knew the difference. Poor sis! She
married a terrible oil can! But she didn't have the looks to get
a real somebody. I'm making this for her. It's a bridge table cover
for her birthday. She'll be twenty-nine. Don't that seem
old?"

"Maybe to you; not to me," said the man in bed.

"You're about forty, aren't you?" said Miss Lyons.

"Just about."

"And how old would you say I am?"

"Twenty-three."

"I'm twenty-five," said Miss Lyons. "Twenty-five and forty.
That's fifteen years' difference. But I know a married couple
that the husband is forty-five and she's only twenty-four, and
they get along fine."

"I'm married myself," said the man in bed.

"You would be!" said Miss Lyons. "The last four cases I've
been on was all married men. But at that, I'd rather have any

kind of a man than a woman. I hate women! I mean sick ones.
They treat a nurse like a dog, especially a pretty nurse. What's
that you're reading?"

" 'Vanity Fair,' " replied the man in bed.

" 'Vanity Fair.' I thought that was a magazine."

"Well, there's a magazine *and* a book. This is the book."

"Is it about a girl?"

"Yes."

"I haven't read it yet. I've been busy making this thing for
my sister's birthday. She'll be twenty-nine. It's a bridge table
cover. When you get that old, about all there is left is bridge or
cross-word puzzles. Are you a puzzle fan? I did them religiously
for a while, but I got sick of them. They put in such crazy words.
Like one day they had a word with only three letters and it
said 'A e-longated fish' and the first letter had to be an *e*. And
only three letters. That *couldn't* be right. So I said if they put
things wrong like that, what's the use? Life's too short. And we
only live once. When you're dead, you stay a long time dead.

"That's what a B. F. of mine used to say. He was a caution!
But he was crazy about me. I might of married him only for a
G. F. telling him lies about me. And called herself my friend!
Charley Pierce."

"Who's Charley Pierce?"

"That was my B. F. that the other girl lied to him about me.
I told him, I said, 'Well, if you believe all them stories about me,
maybe we better part once and for all. I don't want to be tied
up to a somebody that believes all the dirt they hear about me.'
So he said he didn't really believe it and if I would take him back
he wouldn't quarrel with me no more. But I said I thought it was
best for us to part. I got their announcement two years ago, while
I was still in training in Baltimore."

"Did he marry the girl that lied to him about you?"

"Yes, the poor fish! And I bet he's satisfied! They're a match
for each other! He was all right, though, at that, till he fell for

her. He used to be so thoughtful of me, like I was his sister or
something.

"I like a man to respect me. Most fellas wants to kiss you before they know your name.

"Golly! I'm sleepy this morning! And got a right to be, too.
Do you know what time I got home last night, or this morning,
rather? Well, it was half past three. What would mama say if she
could see her little girl now! But we did have a good time. First
we went to the show—'What Price Glory?'—I and my G. F.—
and afterwards her B. F. met us and took us in a taxi down to Barney Gallant's. Peewee Byers has got the orchestra there now.
Used to be with Whiteman's. Gee! How he can dance! I mean
Roy."

"Your G. F.'s B. F.?"

"Yes, but I don't believe he's as crazy about her as she thinks
he is. Anyway—but this is a secret—he took down the phone
number of the hospital while Marian was out powdering her nose,
and he said he'd give me a ring about noon. Gee! I'm sleepy! Roy
Stewart!"

"Well," said Miss Lyons, "how's my patient? I'm twenty minutes late, but honest, it's a wonder I got up at all! Two nights in
succession is too much for this child!"

"Barney Gallant's again?" asked the man in bed.

"No, but it was dancing, and pretty near as late. It'll be different tonight. I'm going to bed just the minute I get home. But I
did have a dandy time. And I'm crazy about a certain somebody."

"Roy Stewart?"

"How'd you guess it? But honest, he's wonderful! And so different than most of the fellas I've met. He says the craziest things,
just keeps you in hysterics. We were talking about books and
reading, and he asked me if I liked poetry—only he called it
'poultry'—and I said I was wild about it and Edgar M. Guest was
just about my favorite, and then I asked him if he liked Kipling

and what do you think he said? He said he didn't know; he'd never kipled.

"He's a scream! We just sat there in the house till half past eleven and didn't do nothing but just talk and the time went like we was at a show. He's better than a show. But finally I noticed how late it was and I asked him didn't he think he better be going and he said he'd go if I'd go with him, so I asked him where could we go at that hour of the night, and he said he knew a roadhouse just a little ways away, and I didn't want to go, but he said we wouldn't stay for only just one dance, so I went with him. To the Jericho Inn.

"I don't know what the woman thought of me where I stay, going out that time of night. But he *is* such a wonderful dancer and such a perfect gentleman! Of course we had more than one dance and it was after two o'clock before I knew it. We had some gin, too, but he just kissed me once and that was when we said good night."

"What about your G. F., Marian? Does she know?"

"About Roy and I? No. I always say that what a person don't know don't hurt them. Besides, there's nothing *for* her to know —yet. But listen: If there was a chance in the world for her, if I thought he cared anything about her, I'd be the last one in the world to accept his intentions. I hope I'm not that kind! But as far as anything serious between them is concerned, well, it's cold. I happen to *know* that. She's not the girl for him.

"In the first place, while she's pretty in a way, her complexion's bad and her hair's scraggy and her figure, well, it's like some woman in the funny pictures. And she's not peppy enough for Roy. She'd rather stay home than do anything. Stay home! It'll be time enough for that when you can't get somebody to take you out.

"She'd never make a wife for him. He'll be a rich man in another year; that is, if things go right for him in Wall Street like he expects. And a man as rich as he'll be wants a wife that can

live up to it and entertain and step out once in a while. He don't
want a wife that's a drag on him. And he's too good-looking for
Marian. A fella as good-looking as him needs a pretty wife or
the first thing you know some girl that is pretty will steal him
off of you. But it's silly to talk about them marrying each other.
He'd have to ask her first, and he's not going to. I know! So I
don't feel at all like I'm trespassing.

"Anyway, you know the old saying, everything goes in love.
And I—— But I'm keeping you from reading your book. Oh,
yes; I almost forgot a T. L. that Miss Halsey said about you. Do
you know what a T. L. is?"

"Yes."

"Well, then, you give me one and I'll give you this one."

"But I haven't talked to anybody but the Doctor. I can give
you one from myself. He asked me how I liked you and I said
all right."

"Well, that's better than nothing. Here's what Miss Halsey
said: She said if you were shaved and fixed up, you wouldn't be
bad. And now I'm going out and see if there's any mail for me.
Most of my mail goes to where I live, but some of it comes here
sometimes. What I'm looking for is a letter from the state board
telling me if I passed my state examination. They ask you the
craziest questions. Like 'Is ice a disinfectant?' Who cares! Nobody's going to waste ice to kill germs when there's so much
of it needed in high-balls. Do you like high-balls? Roy says it
spoils whisky to mix it with water. He takes it straight. He's a
terror! But maybe you want to read."

"Good morning," said Miss Lyons. "Did you sleep good?"

"Not so good," said the man in bed. "I——"

"I bet you got more sleep than I did," said Miss Lyons. "He's
the most persistent somebody I ever knew! I asked him last
night, I said, 'Don't you never get tired of dancing?' So he said,

well, he did get tired of dancing with some people, but there was others who he never got tired of dancing with them. So I said, 'Yes, Mr. Jollier, but I wasn't born yesterday and I know apple sauce when I hear it and I bet you've told that to fifty girls,' I guess he really did mean it, though.

"Of course most anybody'd rather dance with slender girls than stout girls. I remember a B. F. I had one time in Washington. He said dancing with me was just like dancing with nothing. That sounds like he was insulting me, but it was really a compliment. He meant it wasn't any effort to dance with me like with some girls. You take Marian, for instance, and while I'm crazy about her, still that don't make her a good dancer and dancing with her must be a good deal like moving the piano or something.

"I'd die if I was fat! People are always making jokes about fat people. And there's the old saying, 'Nobody loves a fat man'. And it's even worse with a girl. Besides people making jokes about them and don't want to dance with them and so forth, besides that they're always trying to reduce and can't eat what they want to. I bet, though, if I was fat, I'd eat everything in sight. Though I guess not, either. Because I hardly eat anything as it is. But they do make jokes about them.

"I'll never forget one day last winter, I was on a case in Great Neck and the man's wife was the fattest thing! So they had a radio in the house and one day she saw in the paper where Bugs Baer was going to talk on the radio and it would probably be awfully funny because he writes so crazy. Do you ever read his articles? But this woman, she was awfully sensitive about being fat and I nearly died sitting there with her listening to Bugs Baer, because his whole talk was all about some fat woman and he said the craziest things, but I couldn't laugh on account of she being there in the room with me. One thing he said was that the woman, this woman he was talking about, he said she was so fat that she wore a wrist watch on her thumb. Henry J. Belden."

"Who is Henry J. Belden? Is that the name of Bugs Baer's fat lady?"

"No, you crazy!" said Miss Lyons. "Mr. Belden was the case I was on in Great Neck. He died."

"It seems to me a good many of your cases die."

"Isn't it a scream!" said Miss Lyons. "But it's true; that is, it's been true lately. The last five cases I've been on has all died. Of course it's just luck, but the girls have been kidding me about it and calling me a jinx, and when Miss Halsey saw me here the evening of the day you was operated, she said, 'God help him!' That's the night floor nurse's name. But you're going to be mean and live through it and spoil my record, aren't you? I'm just kidding. Of course I want you to get all right.

"But it *is* queer, the way things have happened, and it's made me feel kind of creepy. And besides, I'm not like some of the girls and don't care. I get awfully fond of some of my cases and I hate to see them die, especially if they're men and not very sick and treat you half-way decent and don't yell for you the minute you go out of the room. There's only one case I was ever on where I didn't mind her dying and that was a woman. She had nephritis. Mrs. Judson.

"Do you want some gum? I chew it just when I'm nervous. And I always get nervous when I don't have enough sleep. You can bet I'll stay home tonight, B. F. or no B. F. But anyway he's got an engagement tonight, some directors' meeting or something. He's the busiest somebody in the world. And I told him last night, I said, 'I should think you'd need sleep, too, even more than I do because you have to have all your wits about you in your business or those big bankers would take advantage and rob you. You can't afford to be sleepy,' I told him.

"So he said, 'No, but of course it's all right for you, because if you go to sleep on your job, there's no danger of you doing any damage except maybe give one of your patients a bicholoride of

mercury tablet instead of an alcohol rub.' He's terrible! But you
can't help from laughing.

"There was four of us in the party last night. He brought
along his B. F. and another girl. She was just blah, but the B. F.
wasn't so bad, only he insisted on me helping him drink a half
a bottle of Scotch, and on top of gin, too. I guess I was the life of
the party; that is, at first. Afterwards I got sick and it wasn't so
good.

"But at first I was certainly going strong. And I guess I made
quite a hit with Roy's B. F. He knows Marian, too, but he won't
say anything, and if he does, I don't care. If she don't want to
lose her beaus, she ought to know better than to introduce them
to all the pretty girls in the world. I don't mean that I'm any
Norma Talmadge, but at least—well—but I sure was sick when I
was sick!

"I must give Marian a ring this noon. I haven't talked to her
since the night she introduced me to him. I've been kind of
scared. But I've got to find out what she knows. Or if she's
sore at me. Though I don't see how she can be, do you? But
maybe you want to read."

"I called Marian up, but I didn't get her. She's out of town but
she'll be back tonight. She's been out on a case. Hudson, New
York. That's where she went. The message was waiting for her
when she got home the other night, the night she introduced me
to Roy."

"Good morning," said Miss Lyons.

"Good morning," said the man in bed. "Did you sleep
enough?"

"Yes," said Miss Lyons. "I mean no, not enough."

"Your eyes look bad. They almost look as if you'd been cry-
ing."

"Who? Me? It'd take more than—I mean, I'm not a baby! But go on and read your book."

"Well, good morning," said Miss Lyons. "And how's my patient? And this is the last morning I can call you that, isn't it? I think you're mean to get well so quick and leave me out of a job. I'm just kidding. I'm glad you're all right again, and I can use a little rest myself."

"Another big night?" asked the man in bed.

"Pretty big," said Miss Lyons. "And another one coming. But tomorrow I won't ever get up. Honest, I danced so much last night that I thought my feet would drop off. But he certainly is a dancing fool! And the nicest somebody to talk to that I've met since I came to this town. Not a smart Alex and not always trying to be funny like some people, but just nice. He understands. He seems to know just what you're thinking. George Morse."

"George Morse!" exclaimed the man in bed.

"Why yes," said Miss Lyons. "Do you know him?"

"No. But I thought you were talking about this Stewart, this Roy."

"Oh, him!" said Miss Lyons. "I should say not! He's private property; other people's property, not mine. He's engaged to my G. F. Marian. It happened day before yesterday, after she got home from Hudson. She was on a case up there. She told me about it night before last. I told her congratulations. Because I wouldn't hurt her feelings for the world! But heavens! what a mess she's going to be in, married to that dumb-bell. But of course some people can't be choosey. And I doubt if they ever get married unless some friend loans him the price of a license.

"He's got her believing he's in Wall Street, but I bet if he ever goes there at all, it's to sweep it. He's one of these kind of fellas that's got a great line for a little while, but you don't want to live with a clown. And I'd hate to marry a man that all he thinks about is to step out every night and dance and drink.

"I had a notion to tell her what I really thought. But that'd only of made her sore, or she'd of thought I was jealous or something. As if I couldn't of had him myself! Though even if he wasn't so awful, if I'd liked him instead of loathed him, I wouldn't of taken him from her on account of she being my G. F. And especially while she was out of town.

"He's the kind of a fella that'd marry a nurse in the hopes that some day he'd be an invalid. You know, that kind.

"But say—did you ever hear of J. P. Morgan and Company? That's where my B. F. works, and he don't claim to own it neither. George Morse.

"Haven't you finished that book yet?"

CHAMPION

Midge Kelly scored his first knockout when he was seventeen. The knockee was his brother Connie, three years his junior and a cripple. The purse was a half dollar given to the younger Kelly by a lady whose electric had just missed bumping his soul from his frail little body.

Connie did not know Midge was in the house, else he never would have risked laying the prize on the arm of the least comfortable chair in the room, the better to observe its shining beauty. As Midge entered from the kitchen, the crippled boy covered the coin with his hand, but the movement lacked the speed requisite to escape his brother's quick eye.

"Watcha got there?" demanded Midge.

"Nothin'," said Connie.

"You're a one legged liar!" said Midge.

He strode over to his brother's chair and grasped the hand that concealed the coin.

"Let loose!" he ordered.

Connie began to cry.

"Let loose and shut up your noise," said the elder, and jerked his brother's hand from the chair arm.

The coin fell onto the bare floor. Midge pounced on it. His weak mouth widened in a triumphant smile.

"Nothin', huh?" he said. "All right, if it's nothin' you don't want it."

"Give that back," sobbed the younger.

"I'll give you a red nose, you little sneak! Where'd you steal it?"

"I didn't steal it. It's mine. A lady give it to me after she pretty near hit me with a car."

"It's a crime she missed you," said Midge.

Midge started for the front door. The cripple picked up his crutch, rose from his chair with difficulty, and, still sobbing, came toward Midge. The latter heard him and stopped.

"You better stay where you're at," he said.

"I want my money," cried the boy.

"I know what you want," said Midge.

Doubling up the fist that held the half dollar, he landed with all his strength on his brother's mouth. Connie fell to the floor with a thud, the crutch tumbling on top of him. Midge stood beside the prostrate form.

"Is that enough?" he said. "Or do you want this, too?"

And he kicked him in the crippled leg.

"I guess that'll hold you," he said.

There was no response from the boy on the floor. Midge looked at him a moment, then at the coin in his hand, and then went out into the street, whistling.

An hour later, when Mrs. Kelly came home from her day's work at Faulkner's Steam Laundry, she found Connie on the floor, moaning. Dropping on her knees beside him, she called him by name a score of times. Then she got up and, pale as a ghost, dashed from the house. Dr. Ryan left the Kelly abode about dusk and walked toward Halsted Street. Mrs. Dorgan spied him as he passed her gate.

"Who's sick, Doctor?" she called.

"Poor little Connie," he replied. "He had a bad fall."

"How did it happen?"

"I can't say for sure, Margaret, but I'd almost bet he was knocked down."

"Knocked down!" exclaimed Mrs. Dorgan.

"Why, who—?"

"Have you seen the other one lately?"

"Michael? No, not since mornin'. You can't be thinkin'——"

"I wouldn't put it past him, Margaret," said the doctor gravely. "The lad's mouth is swollen and cut, and his poor, skinny little leg is bruised. He surely didn't do it to himself and I think Ellen suspects the other one."

"Lord save us!" said Mrs. Dorgan. "I'll run over and see if I can help."

"That's a good woman," said Doctor Ryan, and went on down the street.

Near midnight, when Midge came home, his mother was sitting at Connie's bedside. She did not look up.

"Well," said Midge, "what's the matter?"

She remained silent. Midge repeated his question.

"Michael, you know what's the matter," she said at length.

"I don't know nothin'," said Midge.

"Don't lie to me, Michael. What did you do to your brother?"

"Nothin'."

"You hit him."

"Well, then, I hit him. What of it? It ain't the first time."

Her lips pressed tightly together, her face like chalk, Ellen Kelly rose from her chair and made straight for him. Midge backed against the door.

"Lay off'n me, Ma. I don't want to fight no woman."

Still she came on breathing heavily.

"Stop where you're at, Ma," he warned.

There was a brief struggle and Midge's mother lay on the floor before him.

"You ain't hurt, Ma. You're lucky I didn't land good. And I told you to lay off'n me."

"God forgive you, Michael!"

Midge found Hap Collins in the showdown game at the Royal.

"Come on out a minute," he said.

Hap followed him out on the walk.

"I'm leavin' town for a w'ile," said Midge.

"What for?"

"Well, we had a little run-in up to the house. The kid stole a half buck off'n me, and when I went after it he cracked me with his crutch. So I nailed him. And the old lady came at me with a chair and I took it off'n her and she fell down."

"How is Connie hurt?"

"Not bad."

"What are you runnin' away for?"

"Who the hell said I was runnin' away? I'm sick and tired o' gettin' picked on; that's all. So I'm leavin' for a w'ile and I want a piece o' money."

"I ain't only got six bits," said Happy.

"You're in bad shape, ain't you? Well, come through with it."

Happy came through.

"You oughtn't to hit the kid," he said.

"I ain't astin' you who can I hit," snarled Midge. "You try to put somethin' over on me and you'll get the same dose. I'm goin' now."

"Go as far as you like," said Happy, but not until he was sure that Kelly was out of hearing.

Early the following morning, Midge boarded a train for Milwaukee. He had no ticket, but no one knew the difference. The conductor remained in the caboose.

On a night six months later, Midge hurried out of the "stage door" of the Star Boxing Club and made for Duane's saloon, two blocks away. In his pocket were twelve dollars, his reward for having battered up one Demon Dempsey through the six rounds of the first preliminary.

It was Midge's first professional engagement in the manly art. Also it was the first time in weeks that he had earned twelve dollars.

On the way to Duane's he had to pass Niemann's. He pulled
his cap over his eyes and increased his pace until he had gone by.
Inside Niemann's stood a trusting bartender, who for ten days
had staked Midge to drinks and allowed him to ravage the lunch
on a promise to come in and settle the moment he was paid for
the "prelim."

Midge strode into Duane's and aroused the napping bartender
by slapping a silver dollar on the festive board.

"Gimme a shot," said Midge.

The shooting continued until the wind-up at the Star was over
and part of the fight crowd joined Midge in front of Duane's bar.
A youth in the early twenties, standing next to young Kelly,
finally summoned sufficient courage to address him.

"Wasn't you in the first bout?" he ventured.

"Yeh," Midge replied.

"My name's Hersch," said the other.

Midge received the startling information in silence.

"I don't want to butt in," continued Mr. Hersch, "but I'd like
to buy you a drink."

"All right," said Midge, "but don't overstrain yourself."

Mr. Hersch laughed uproariously and beckoned to the bartender.

"You certainly gave that wop a trimmin' tonight," said the
buyer of the drink, when they had been served. "I thought you'd
kill him."

"I would if I hadn't let up," Midge replied. "I'll kill 'em all."

"You got the wallop all right," the other said admiringly.

"Have I got the wallop?" said Midge. "Say, I can kick like a
mule. Did you notice them muscles in my shoulders?"

"Notice 'em? I couldn't help from noticin' 'em," said Hersch.
"I says to the fella settin' alongside o' me, I says: 'Look at them
shoulders! No wonder he can hit,' I says to him."

"Just let me land and it's good-by, baby," said Midge. "I'll kill
'em all."

The oral manslaughter continued until Duane's closed for the night. At parting, Midge and his new friend shook hands and arranged for a meeting the following evening.

For nearly a week the two were together almost constantly. It was Hersch's pleasant rôle to listen to Midge's modest revelations concerning himself, and to buy every time Midge's glass was empty. But there came an evening when Hersch regretfully announced that he must go home to supper.

"I got a date for eight bells," he confided. "I could stick till then, only I must clean up and put on the Sunday clo'es, 'cause she's the prettiest little thing in Milwaukee."

"Can't you fix it for two?" asked Midge.

"I don't know who to get," Hersch replied. "Wait, though. I got a sister and if she ain't busy, it'll be O. K. She's no bum for looks herself."

So it came about that Midge and Emma Hersch and Emma's brother and the prettiest little thing in Milwaukee foregathered at Wall's and danced half the night away. And Midge and Emma danced every dance together, for though every little onestep seemed to induce a new thirst of its own, Lou Hersch stayed too sober to dance with his own sister.

The next day, penniless at last in spite of his phenomenal ability to make someone else settle, Midge Kelly sought out Doc Hammond, matchmaker for the Star, and asked to be booked for the next show.

"I could put you on with Tracy for the next bout," said Doc.

"What's they in it?" asked Midge.

"Twenty if you cop," Doc told him.

"Have a heart," protested Midge. "Didn't I look good the other night?"

"You looked all right. But you aren't Freddie Welsh yet by a consid'able margin."

"I ain't scared of Freddie Welsh or none of 'em," said Midge.

"Well, we don't pay our boxers by the size of their chests,"

Doc said. "I'm offerin' you this Tracy bout. Take it or leave it."

"All right; I'm on," said Midge, and he passed a pleasant afternoon at Duane's on the strength of his booking.

Young Tracy's manager came to Midge the night before the show.

"How do you feel about this go?" he asked.

"Me?" said Midge, "I feel all right. What do you mean, how do I feel?"

"I mean," said Tracy's manager, "that we're mighty anxious to win, 'cause the boy's got a chanct in Philly if he cops this one."

"What's your proposition?" asked Midge.

"Fifty bucks," said Tracy's manager.

"What do you think I am, a crook? Me lay down for fifty bucks. Not me!"

"Seventy-five, then," said Tracy's manager.

The market closed on eighty and the details were agreed on in short order. And the next night Midge was stopped in the second round by a terrific slap on the forearm.

This time Midge passed up both Niemann's and Duane's, having a sizable account at each place, and sought his refreshment at Stein's farther down the street.

When the profits of his deal with Tracy were gone, he learned, by first-hand information from Doc Hammond and the matchmakers at other "clubs," that he was no longer desired for even the cheapest of preliminaries. There was no danger of his starving or dying of thirst while Emma and Lou Hersch lived. But he made up his mind, four months after his defeat by Young Tracy, that Milwaukee was not the ideal place for him to live.

"I can lick the best of 'em," he reasoned, "but there ain't no more chanct for me here. I can maybe go east and get on somewheres. And besides——"

But just after Midge had purchased a ticket to Chicago with the money he had "borrowed" from Emma Hersch "to buy shoes," a heavy hand was laid on his shoulders and he turned to face two strangers.

"Where are you goin', Kelly?" inquired the owner of the heavy hand.

"Nowheres," said Midge. "What the hell do you care?"

The other stranger spoke:

"Kelly, I'm employed by Emma Hersch's mother to see that you do right by her. And we want you to stay here till you've done it."

"You won't get nothin' but the worst of it, monkeying with me," said Midge.

Nevertheless he did not depart for Chicago that night. Two days later, Emma Hersch became Mrs. Kelly, and the gift of the groom, when once they were alone, was a crushing blow on the bride's pale cheek.

Next morning, Midge left Milwaukee as he had entered it— by fast freight.

"They's no use kiddin' ourself any more," said Tommy Haley. "He might get down to thirty-seven in a pinch, but if he done below that a mouse could stop him. He's a welter; that's what he is and he knows it as well as I do. He's growed like a weed in the last six mont's. I told him, I says, 'If you don't quit growin' they won't be nobody for you to box, only Willard and them.' He says, 'Well, I wouldn't run away from Willard if I weighed twenty pounds more.'"

"He must hate himself," said Tommy's brother.

"I never seen a good one that didn't," said Tommy. "And Midge is a good one; don't make no mistake about that. I wisht we could of got Welsh before the kid growed so big. But it's too late now. I won't make no holler, though, if we can match him up with the Dutchman."

"Who do you mean?"

"Young Goetz, the welter champ. We mightn't not get so

much dough for the bout itself, but it'd roll in afterward. What
a drawin' card we'd be, 'cause the people pays their money to
see the fella with the wallop, and that's Midge. And we'd keep
the title just as long as Midge could make the weight."

"Can't you land no match with Goetz?"

"Sure, 'cause he needs the money. But I've went careful with
the kid so far and look at the results I got! So what's the use of
takin' a chanct? The kid's comin' every minute and Goetz is
goin' back fastern' big Johnson did. I think we could lick him
now; I'd bet my life on it. But six mont's from now they won't
be no risk. He'll of licked hisself before that time. Then all as
we'll have to do is sign up with him and wait for the referee to
stop it. But Midge is so crazy to get at him now that I can't hardly
hold him back."

The brothers Haley were lunching in a Boston hotel. Dan had
come down from Holyoke to visit with Tommy and to watch
the latter's protégeé go twelve rounds, or less, with Bud Cross.
The bout promised little in the way of a contest, for Midge had
twice stopped the Baltimore youth and Bud's reputation for
gameness was all that had earned him the date. The fans were
willing to pay the price to see Midge's hay-making left, but they
wanted to see it used on an opponent who would not jump out
of the ring the first time he felt its crushing force. Bud Cross was
such an opponent, and his willingness to stop boxing-gloves with
his eyes, ears, nose and throat had long enabled him to escape
the horrors of honest labor. A game boy was Bud, and he showed
it in his battered, swollen, discolored face.

"I should think," said Dan Haley, "that the kid'd do whatever
you tell him after all you done for him."

"Well," said Tommy, "he's took my dope pretty straight so
far, but he's so sure of hisself that he can't see no reason for
waitin'. He'll do what I say, though; he'd be a sucker not to."

"You got a contrac' with him?"

"No, I don't need no contrac'. He knows it was me that drug

him out o' the gutter and he ain't goin' to turn me down now, when he's got the dough and bound to get more. Where'd he of been at if I hadn't listened to him when he first come to me? That's pretty near two years ago now, but it seems like last week. I was settin' in the s'loon acrost from the Pleasant Club in Philly, waitin' for McCann to count the dough and come over, when this little bum blowed in and tried to stand the house off for a drink. They told him nothin' doin' and to beat it out o' there, and then he seen me and come over to where I was settin' and ast me wasn't I a boxin' man and I told him who I was. Then he ast me for money to buy a shot and I told him to set down and I'd buy it for him.

"Then we got talkin' things over and he told me his name and told me about fightin' a couple o' prelims out to Milwaukee. So I says, 'Well, boy, I don't know how good or how rotten you are, but you won't never get nowheres trainin' on that stuff.' So he says he'd cut it out if he could get on in a bout and I says I would give him a chanct if he played square with me and didn't touch no more to drink. So we shook hands and I took him up to the hotel with me and give him a bath and the next day I bought him some clo'es. And I staked him to eats and sleeps for over six weeks. He had a hard time breakin' away from the polish, but finally I thought he was fit and I give him his chanct. He went on with Smiley Sayer and stopped him so quick that Smiley thought sure he was poisoned.

"Well, you know what he'd did since. The only beatin' in his record was by Tracy in Milwaukee before I got hold of him, and he's licked Tracy three times in the last year.

"I've gave him all the best of it in a money way and he's got seven thousand bucks in cold storage. How's that for a kid that was in the gutter two years ago? And he'd have still more yet if he wasn't so nuts over clo'es and got to stop at the good hotels and so forth."

"Where's his home at?"

"Well, he ain't really got no home. He came from Chicago and his mother canned him out o' the house for bein' no good. She give him a raw deal, I guess, and he says he won't have nothin' to do with her unlest she comes to him first. She's got a pile o' money, he says, so he ain't worryin' about her."

The gentleman under discussion entered the café and swaggered to Tommy's table, while the whole room turned to look.

Midge was the picture of health despite a slightly colored eye and an ear that seemed to have no opening. But perhaps it was not his healthiness that drew all eyes. His diamond horse-shoe tie pin, his purple cross-striped shirt, his orange shoes and his light blue suit fairly screamed for attention.

"Where you been?" he asked Tommy. "I been lookin' all over for you."

"Set down," said his manager.

"No time," said Midge. "I'm goin' down to the w'arf and see 'em unload the fish."

"Shake hands with my brother Dan," said Tommy.

Midge shook hands with the Holyoke Haley.

"If you're Tommy's brother, you're O.K. with me," said Midge, and the brothers beamed with pleasure.

Dan moistened his lips and murmured an embarrassed reply, but it was lost on the young gladiator.

"Leave me take twenty," Midge was saying. "I prob'ly won't need it, but I don't like to be caught short.'

Tommy parted with a twenty dollar bill and recorded the transaction in a small black book the insurance company had given him for Christmas.

"But," he said, "It won't cost you no twenty to look at them fish. Want me to go along?"

"No," said Midge hastily. "You and your brother here prob'ly got a lot to say to each other."

"Well," said Tommy, "don't take no bad money and don't get

lost. And you better be back at four o'clock and lay down a w'ile."

"I don't need no rest to beat this guy," said Midge. "He'll do enough layin' down for the both of us."

And laughing even more than the jest called for, he strode out through the fire of admiring and startled glances.

The corner of Boylston and Tremont was the nearest Midge got to the wharf, but the lady awaiting him was doubtless a more dazzling sight than the catch of the luckiest Massachusetts fisherman. She could talk, too—probably better than the fish.

"O you Kid!" she said, flashing a few silver teeth among the gold. "O you fighting man!"

Midge smiled up at her.

"We'll go somewheres and get a drink," he said. "One won't hurt."

In New Orleans, five months after he had rearranged the map of Bud Cross for the third time, Midge finished training for his championship bout with the Dutchman.

Back in his hotel after the final workout, Midge stopped to chat with some of the boys from up north, who had made the long trip to see a champion dethroned, for the result of this bout was so nearly a foregone conclusion that even the experts had guessed it.

Tommy Haley secured the key and the mail and ascended to the Kelly suite. He was bathing when Midge came in, half an hour later.

"Any mail?" asked Midge.

"There on the bed," replied Tommy from the tub.

Midge picked up the stack of letters and postcards and glanced them over. From the pile he sorted out three letters and laid them on the table. The rest he tossed into the waste-basket. Then he picked up the three and sat for a few moments holding them, while his eyes gazed off into space. At length he looked again at the three unopened letters in his hand; then he put one in his pocket and tossed the other two at the basket. They missed their target and fell on the floor.

"Hell!" said Midge, and stooping over picked them up.

He opened one postmarked Milwaukee and read:

Dear Husband:

I have wrote to you so manny times and got no anser and I dont know if you ever got them, so I am writeing again in the hopes you will get this letter and anser. I dont like to bother you with my trubles and I would not only for the baby and I am not asking you should write to me but only send a little money and I am not asking for myself but the baby has not been well a day sence last Aug. and the dr. told me she cant live much longer unless I give her better food and thats impossible the ways things are. Lou has not been working for a year and what I make dont hardley pay for the rent. I am not asking for you to give me any money, but only you should send what I loaned when convenient and I think it amts. to about $36.00. Please try and send that amt. and it will help me, but if you cant send the whole amt. try and send me something.

Your wife,
EMMA.

Midge tore the letter into a hundred pieces and scattered them over the floor.

"Money, money, money!" he said. "They must think I'm made o' money. I s'pose the old woman's after it too."

He opened his mother's letter:

dear Michael Connie wonted me to rite and say you must beet the dutchman and he is sur you will and wonted me to say we wont you to rite and tell us about it, but I gess you havent no time to rite or we herd from you long beffore this but I wish you would rite jest a line or 2 boy becaus it wuld be better for Connie then a barl of medisin. It wuld help me to keep things going if you send me money now and then when you can spair it but if you cant send no money try and fine time to rite a letter onley a few lines and it will please Connie, jest think boy he hasent got out of bed in over 3 yrs. Connie says good luck.

Your Mother,
ELLEN F. KELLY.

"I thought so," said Midge. "They're all alike."
The third letter was from New York. It read:

Hon:—This is the last letter you will get from me before your champ, but I will send you a telegram Saturday, but I can't say as much in a telegram as in a letter and I am writeing this to let you know I am thinking of you and praying for good luck.

Lick him good hon and don't wait no longer than you have to and don't forget to wire me as soon as its over. Give him that little old left of yours on the nose hon and don't be afraid of spoiling his good looks because he couldn't be no homlier than he is. But don't let him spoil my baby's pretty face. You won't will you hon.

Well hon I would give anything to be there and see it, but I guess you love Haley better than me or you wouldn't let him keep me away. But when your champ hon we can do as we please and tell Haley to go to the devil.

Well hon I will send you a telegram Saturday and I almost forgot to tell you I will need some more money, a couple hundred say and you will have to wire it to me as soon as you get this. You will won't you hon.

I will send you a telegram Saturday and remember hon I am pulling for you.

Well good-by sweetheart and good luck.

GRACE.

"They're all alike," said Midge. "Money, money, money."
Tommy Haley, shining from his ablutions, came in from the adjoining room.

"Thought you'd be layin' down," he said.

"I'm goin' to," said Midge, unbuttoning his orange shoes.

"I'll call you at six and you can eat up here without no bugs to pester you. I got to go down and give them birds their tickets."

"Did you hear from Goldberg?" asked Midge.

"Didn't I tell you? Sure; fifteen weeks at five hundred, if we win. And we can get a guarantee o' twelve thousand, with privileges either in New York or Milwaukee."

"Who with?"

"Anybody that'll stand up in front of you. You don't care who it is, do you?"

"Not me. I'll make 'em all look like a monkey."

"Well you better lay down aw'ile."

"Oh, say, wire two hundred to Grace for me, will you? Right away; the New York address."

"Two hundred! You just sent her three hundred last Sunday."

"Well, what the hell do you care?"

"All right, all right. Don't get sore about it. Anything else?"

"That's all," said Midge, and dropped onto the bed.

"And I want the deed done before I come back," said Grace as she rose from the table. "You won't fall down on me, will you, hon?"

"Leave it to me," said Midge. "And don't spend no more than you have to."

Grace smiled a farewell and left the café. Midge continued to sip his coffee and read his paper.

They were in Chicago and they were in the middle of Midge's first week in vaudeville. He had come straight north to reap the rewards of his glorious victory over the broken down Dutchman. A fortnight had been spent in learning his act, which consisted of a gymnastic exhibition and a ten minutes' monologue on the various excellences of Midge Kelly. And now he was twice daily turning 'em away from the Madison Theater.

His breakfast over and his paper read, Midge sauntered into

the lobby and asked for his key. He then beckoned to a bell-boy, who had been hoping for that very honor.

"Find Haley, Tommy Haley," said Midge. "Tell him to come up to my room."

"Yes, sir, Mr. Kelly," said the boy, and proceeded to break all his former records for diligence.

Midge was looking out of his seventh-story window when Tommy answered the summons.

"What'll it be?" inquired his manager.

There was a pause before Midge replied.

"Haley," he said, "twenty-five per cent's a whole lot o' money."

"I guess I got it comin', ain't I?" said Tommy.

"I don't see how you figger it. I don't see where you're worth it to me."

"Well," said Tommy, "I didn't expect nothin' like this. I thought you was satisfied with the bargain. I don't want to beat nobody out o' nothin', but I don't see where you could have got anybody else that would of did all I done for you."

"Sure, that's all right," said the champion. "You done a lot for me in Philly. And you got good money for it, didn't you?"

"I ain't makin' no holler. Still and all, the big money's still ahead of us yet. And if it hadn't of been for me, you wouldn't of never got within grabbin' distance."

"Oh, I guess I could of went along all right," said Midge. "Who was it that hung that left on the Dutchman's jaw, me or you?"

"Yes, but you wouldn't been in the ring with the Dutchman if it wasn't for how I handled you."

"Well, this won't get us nowheres. The idear is that you ain't worth no twenty-five per cent now and it don't make no dif- f'rence what come off a year or two ago."

"Don't it?" said Tommy. "I'd say it made a whole lot of dif- ference."

"Well, I say it don't and I guess that settles it."

"Look here, Midge," Tommy said, "I thought I was fair with you, but if you don't think so, I'm willin' to hear what you think is fair. I don't want nobody callin' me a Sherlock. Let's go down to business and sign up a contrac'. What's your figger?"

"I ain't namin' no figger," Midge replied. "I'm sayin' that twenty-five's too much. Now what are you willin' to take?"

"How about twenty?"

"Twenty's too much," said Kelly.

"What ain't too much?" asked Tommy.

"Well, Haley, I might as well give it to you straight. They ain't nothin' that ain't too much."

"You mean you don't want me at no figger?"

"That's the idear."

There was a minute's silence. Then Tommy Haley walked toward the door.

"Midge," he said, in a choking voice, "you're makin' a big mistake, boy. You can't throw down your best friends and get away with it. That damn woman will ruin you."

Midge sprang from his seat.

"You shut your mouth!" he stormed. "Get out o' here before they have to carry you out. You been spongin' off o' me long enough. Say one more word about the girl or about anything else and you'll get what the Dutchman got. Now get out!"

And Tommy Haley, having a very vivid memory of the Dutchman's face as he fell, got out.

Grace came in later, dropped her numerous bundles on the lounge and perched herself on the arm of Midge's chair.

"Well?" she said.

"Well," said Midge, "I got rid of him."

"Good boy!" said Grace. "And now I think you might give me that twenty-five per cent."

"Besides the seventy-five you're already gettin'?" said Midge.

"Don't be no grouch, hon. You don't look pretty when you're grouchy."

"It ain't my business to look pretty," Midge replied.

"Wait till you see how I look with the stuff I bought this mornin'!"

Midge glanced at the bundles on the lounge.

"There's Haley's twenty-five per cent," he said, "and then some."

The champion did not remain long without a manager. Haley's successor was none other than Jerome Harris, who saw in Midge a better meal ticket than his popular-priced musical show had been.

The contract, giving Mr. Harris twenty-five per cent of Midge's earnings, was signed in Detroit the week after Tommy Haley had heard his dismissal read. It had taken Midge just six days to learn that a popular actor cannot get on without the ministrations of a man who thinks, talks and means business. At first Grace objected to the new member of the firm, but when Mr. Harris had demanded and secured from the vaudeville people a one-hundred dollar increase in Midge's weekly stipend, she was convinced that the champion had acted for the best.

"You and my missus will have some great old times," Harris told Grace. "I'd of wired her to join us here, only I seen the Kid's bookin' takes us to Milwaukee next week, and that's where she is."

But when they were introduced in the Milwaukee hotel, Grace admitted to herself that her feeling for Mrs. Harris could hardly be called love at first sight. Midge, on the contrary, gave his new manager's wife the many times over and seemed loath to end the feast of his eyes.

"Some doll," he said to Grace when they were alone.

"Doll is right," the lady replied, "and sawdust where her brains ought to be."

"I'm li'ble to steal that baby," said Midge, and he smiled as he noted the effect of his words on his audience's face.

On Tuesday of the Milwaukee week the champion successfully defended his title in a bout that the newspapers never reported. Midge was alone in his room that morning when a visitor entered without knocking. The visitor was Lou Hersch.

Midge turned white at sight of him.

"What do you want?" he demanded.

"I guess you know," said Lou Hersch. "Your wife's starvin' to death and your baby's starvin' to death and I'm starvin' to death. And you're dirty with money."

"Listen," said Midge, "if it wasn't for you, I wouldn't never saw your sister. And, if you ain't man enough to hold a job, what's that to me? The best thing you can do is keep away from me."

"You give me a piece o' money and I'll go."

Midge's reply to the ultimatum was a straight right to his brother-in-law's narrow chest.

"Take that home to your sister."

And after Lou Hersch picked himself up and slunk away, Midge thought: "It's lucky I didn't give him my left or I'd of croaked him. And if I'd hit him in the stomach, I'd of broke his spine."

There was a party after each evening performance during the Milwaukee engagement. The wine flowed freely and Midge had more of it than Tommy Haley ever would have permitted him. Mr. Harris offered no objection, which was possibly just as well for his own physical comfort.

In the dancing between drinks, Midge had his new manager's wife for a partner as often as Grace. The latter's face as she floundered round in the arms of the portly Harris, belied her frequent protestations that she was having the time of her life.

Several times that week, Midge thought Grace was on the point of starting the quarrel he hoped to have. But it was not until Friday night that she accommodated. He and Mrs. Harris had disappeared after the matinee and when Grace saw him again at the close of the night show, she came to the point at once.

"What are you tryin' to pull off?" she demanded.

"It's none o' your business, is it?" said Midge.

"You bet it's my business; mine and Harris's. You cut it short or you'll find out."

"Listen," said Midge, "have you got a mortgage on me or somethin'? You talk like we was married."

"We're goin' to be, too. And tomorrow's as good a time as any."

"Just about," Midge said. "You got as much chanct o' marryin' me to-morrow as the next day or next year and that ain't no chanct at all."

"We'll find out," said Grace.

"You're the one that's got somethin' to find out."

"What do you mean?"

"I mean I'm married already."

"You lie!"

"You think so, do you? Well, s'pose you go to this here address and get acquainted with my missus."

Midge scrawled a number on a piece of paper and handed it to her. She stared at it unseeingly.

"Well," said Midge, "I ain't kiddin' you. You go there and ask for Mrs. Michael Kelly, and if you don't find her, I'll marry you to-morrow before breakfast."

Still Grace stared at the scrap of paper. To Midge it seemed an age before she spoke again.

"You lied to me all this w'ile."

"You never ast me was I married. What's more, what the hell diff'rence did it make to you? You got a split, didn't you? Better'n fifty-fifty."

He started away.

"Where you goin'?"

"I'm goin' to meet Harris and his wife."

"I'm goin' with you. You're not goin' to shake me now."

"Yes, I am, too," said Midge quietly. "When I leave town to-morrow night, you're going to stay here. And if I see where you're goin' to make a fuss, I'll put you in a hospital where they'll keep you quiet. You can get your stuff to-morrow mornin' and I'll slip you a hundred bucks. And then I don't want to see no more o' you. And don't try and tag along now or I'll have to add another K. O. to the old record."

When Grace returned to the hotel that night, she discovered that Midge and the Harrises had moved to another. And when Midge left town the following night, he was again without a manager, and Mr. Harris was without a wife.

Three days prior to Midge Kelly's ten-round bout with Young Milton in New York City, the sporting editor of *The News* assigned Joe Morgan to write two or three thousand words about the champion to run with a picture lay-out for Sunday.

Joe Morgan dropped in at Midge's training quarters Friday afternoon. Midge, he learned, was doing road work, but Midge's manager, Wallie Adams, stood ready and willing to supply reams of dope about the greatest fighter of the age.

"Let's hear what you've got," said Joe, "and then I'll try to fix up something."

So Wallie stepped on the accelerator of his imagination and shot away.

"Just a kid; that's all he is; a regular boy. Get what I mean? Don't know the meanin' o' bad habits. Never tasted liquor in his life and would prob'bly get sick if he smelled it. Clean livin' put him up where he's at. Get what I mean? And modest and un-assumin' as a school girl. He's so quiet you wouldn't never know he was round. And he'd go to jail before he'd talk about himself.

"No job at all to get him in shape, 'cause he's always that way. The only trouble we have with him is gettin' him to light into these poor bums they match him up with. He's scared he'll hurt somebody. Get what I mean? He's tickled to death over this match with Milton, 'cause everybody says Milton can stand the gaff. Midge'll maybe be able to cut loose a little this time. But the last two bouts he had, the guys hadn't no business in the ring with him, and he was holdin' back all the w'ile for the fear he'd kill somebody. Get what I mean?"

"Is he married?" inquired Joe.

"Say, you'd think he was married to hear him rave about them kiddies he's got. His fam'ly's up in Canada to their summer home and Midge is wild to get up there with 'em. He thinks more o' that wife and them kiddies than all the money in the world. Get what I mean?"

"How many children has he?"

"I don't know, four or five, I guess. All boys and every one of 'em a dead ringer for their dad."

"Is his father living?"

"No, the old man died when he was a kid. But he's got a grand old mother and a kid brother out in Chi. They're the first ones he thinks about after a match, them and his wife and kiddies. And he don't forget to send the old woman a thousand bucks after every bout. He's goin' to buy her a new home as soon as they pay him off for this match."

"How about his brother? Is he going to tackle the game?"

"Sure, and Midge says he'll be a champion before he's twenty years old. They're a fightin' fam'ly and all of 'em honest and straight as a die. Get what I mean? A fella that I can't tell you his name come to Midge in Milwaukee onct and wanted him to throw a fight and Midge give him such a trimmin' in the street that he couldn't go on that night. That's the kind he is. Get what I mean?"

Joe Morgan hung around the camp until Midge and his trainers returned.

"One o' the boys from *The News*," said Wallie by way of introduction. "I been givin' him your fam'ly hist'ry."

"Did he give you good dope?" he inquired.

"He's some historian," said Joe.

"Don't call me no names," said Wallie smiling. "Call us up if they's anything more you want. And keep your eyes on us Monday night. Get what I mean?"

The story in Sunday's *News* was read by thousands of lovers of the manly art. It was well written and full of human interest. Its slight inaccuracies went unchallenged, though three readers, besides Wallie Adams and Midge Kelly, saw and recognized them. The three were Grace, Tommy Haley and Jerome Harris and the comments they made were not for publication.

Neither the Mrs. Kelly in Chicago nor the Mrs. Kelly in Milwaukee knew that there was such a paper as the New York *News*. And even if they had known of it and that it contained two columns of reading matter about Midge, neither mother nor wife could have bought it. For *The News* on Sunday is a nickel a copy.

Joe Morgan could have written more accurately, no doubt, if instead of Wallie Adams, he had interviewed Ellen Kelly and Connie Kelly and Emma Kelly and Lou Hersch and Grace and Jerome Harris and Tommy Haley and Hap Collins and two or three Milwaukee bartenders.

But a story built on their evidence would never have passed the sporting editor.

"Suppose you can prove it," that gentleman would have said, "It wouldn't get us anything but abuse to print it. The people don't want to see him knocked. He's champion."

A DAY WITH
CONRAD GREEN

Conrad Green woke up depressed and, for a moment, could not think why. Then he remembered. Herman Plant was dead; Herman Plant, who had been his confidential secretary ever since he had begun producing; who had been much more than a secretary —his champion, votary, shield, bodyguard, tool, occasional lackey, and the butt of his heavy jokes and nasty temper. For forty-five dollars a week.

Herman Plant was dead, and this Lewis, recommended by Ezra Peebles, a fellow entrepreneur, had not, yesterday, made a good first impression. Lewis was apparently impervious to hints. You had to tell him things right out, and when he did understand he looked at you as if you were a boob. And insisted on a salary of sixty dollars right at the start. Perhaps Peebles, who, Green knew, hated him almost enough to make it fifty-fifty, was doing him another dirty trick dressed up as a favor.

After ten o'clock, and still Green had not had enough sleep. It had been nearly three when his young wife and he had left the Bryant-Walkers'. Mrs. Green, the former Marjorie Manning of the Vanities chorus, had driven home to Long Island, while he had stayed in the rooms he always kept at the Ambassador.

Marjorie had wanted to leave a good deal earlier; through no lack of effort on her part she had been almost entirely ignored

by her aristocratic host and hostess and most of the guests. She
had confided to her husband more than once that she was sick
of the whole such-and-such bunch of so-and-so's. As far as she
was concerned, they could all go to hell and stay there! But
Green had been rushed by the pretty and stage-struck Joyce
Brainard, wife of the international polo star, and had successfully
combated his own wife's importunities till the Brainards themselves had gone.

Yes, he could have used a little more sleep, but the memory of
the party cheered him. Mrs. Brainard, excited by his theatrical
aura and several highballs, had been almost affectionate. She had
promised to come to his office some time and talk over a stage
career which both knew was impossible so long as Brainard lived.
But, best of all, Mr. and Mrs. Green would be listed in the papers
as among those present at the Bryant-Walkers', along with the
Vanderbecks, the Suttons, and the Schuylers, and that would just
about be the death of Peebles and other social sycophants of
"show business." He would order all the papers now and look
for his name. No; he was late and must get to his office. No telling what a mess things were in without Herman Plant. And, by
the way, he mustn't forget Plant's funeral this afternoon.

He bathed, telephoned for his breakfast, and his favorite barber, dressed in a symphony of purple and gray, and set out for
Broadway, pretending not to hear the "There's Conrad Green!"
spoken in awed tones by two flappers and a Westchester realtor
whom he passed en route.

Green let himself into his private office, an office of luxurious,
exotic furnishings, its walls adorned with expensive landscapes
and a Zuloaga portrait of his wife. He took off his twenty-five
dollar velour hat, approved of himself in the large mirror, sat
down at his desk, and rang for Miss Jackson.

"All the morning papers," he ordered, "and tell Lewis to come
in."

"I'll have to send out for the papers," said Miss Jackson, a tired-looking woman of forty-five or fifty.

"What do you mean, send out? I thought we had an arrangement with that boy to leave them every morning."

"We did. But the boy says he can't leave them any more till we've paid up to date."

"What do we owe?"

"Sixty-five dollars."

"Sixty-five dollars! He's crazy! Haven't you been paying him by the week?"

"No. You told me not to."

"I told you nothing of the kind! Sixty-five dollars! He's trying to rob us!"

"I don't believe so, Mr. Green," said Miss Jackson. "He showed me his book. It's more than thirty weeks since he began, and you know we've never paid him."

"But hell! There isn't sixty-five dollars' worth of newspapers ever been printed! Tell him to sue us! And now send out for the papers and do it quick! After this we'll get them down at the corner every morning and pay for them. Tell Lewis to bring me the mail."

Miss Jackson left him, and presently the new secretary came in. He was a man under thirty, whom one would have taken for a high school teacher rather than a theatrical general's aide-de-camp.

"Good-morning, Mr. Green," he said.

His employer disregarded the greeting.

"Anything in the mail?" he asked.

"Not much of importance. I've already answered most of it. Here are a few things from your clipping bureau and a sort of dunning letter from some jeweler in Philadelphia."

"What did you open that for?" demanded Green, crossly. "Wasn't it marked personal?"

"Look here, Mr. Green," said Lewis quietly: "I was told you had a habit of being rough with your employees. I want to warn you that I am not used to that sort of treatment and don't intend to get used to it. If you are decent with me, I'll work for you. Otherwise I'll resign."

"I don't know what you're talking about, Lewis. I didn't mean to be rough. It's just my way of speaking. Let's forget it and I'll try not to give you any more cause to complain."

"All right, Mr. Green. You told me to open all your mail except the letters with that one little mark on them——"

"Yes, I know. Now let's have the clippings."

Lewis laid them on the desk.

"I threw away about ten of them that were all the same—the announcement that you had signed Bonnie Blue for next season. There's one there that speaks of a possible partnership between you and Sam Stein——"

"What a nerve he's got, giving out a statement like that. Fine chance of me mixing myself up with a crook like Stein! Peebles says he's a full stepbrother to the James boys. So is Peebles himself, for that matter. What's this long one about?"

"It's about that young composer, Casper Ettelson. It's by Deems Taylor of the *World*. There's just a mention of you down at the bottom."

"Read it to me, will you? I've overstrained my eyes lately."

The dead Herman Plant had first heard of that recent eye strain twenty years ago. It amounted to almost total blindness where words of over two syllables were concerned.

"So far," Lewis read, "Ettelson has not had a book worthy of his imaginative, whimsical music. How we would revel in an Ettelson score with a Barrie libretto and a Conrad Green production."

"Who is this Barrie?" asked Green.

"I suppose it's James M. Barrie," replied Lewis, "the man who wrote Peter Pan."

"I thought that was written by a fella over in England," said Green.

"I guess he does live in England. He was born in Scotland. I don't know where he is now."

"Well, find out if he's in New York, and, if he is, get a hold of him. Maybe he'll do a couple of scenes for our next show. Come in, Miss Jackson. Oh, the papers!"

Miss Jackson handed them to him and went out. Green turned first to the society page of the *Herald Tribune*. His eye trouble was not so severe as to prevent his finding that page. And he could read his name when it was there to be read.

Three paragraphs were devoted to the Bryant-Walker affair, two of them being lists of names. And Mr. and Mrs. Conrad Green were left out.

"——!" commented Green, and grabbed the other papers. The *World* and *Times* were searched with the same hideous result. And the others did not mention the party at all.

"——!" repeated Green. "I'll get somebody for this!" Then, to Lewis: "Here! Take this telegram. Send it to the managing editors of all the morning papers; you'll find their names pasted on Plant's desk. Now: 'Ask your society editor why my name was not on list of guests at Bryant-Walker dinner Wednesday night. Makes no difference to me, as am not seeking and do not need publicity, but it looks like conspiracy, and thought you ought to be informed, as have always been good friend of your paper, as well as steady advertiser.' I guess that's enough."

"If you'll pardon a suggestion," said Lewis, "I'm afraid a telegram like this would just be laughed at."

"You send the telegram; I'm not going to have a bunch of cheap reporters make a fool of me!"

"I don't believe you can blame the reporters. There probably weren't reporters there. The list of guests is generally given out by the people who give the party."

"But listen——" Green paused and thought. "All right. Don't

send the telegram. But if the Bryant-Walkers are ashamed of me, why the hell did they invite me? I certainly didn't want to go and they weren't under obligation to me. I never——"

As if it had been waiting for its cue, the telephone rang at this instant, and Kate, the switchboard girl, announced that the Bryant-Walkers' secretary was on the wire.

"I am speaking for Mrs. Bryant-Walker," said a female voice. "She is chairman of the committee on entertainment for the Women's Progress Bazaar. The bazaar is to open on the third of next month and wind up on the evening of the fifth with a sort of vaudeville entertainment. She wanted me to ask you——"

Green hung up with an oath.

"That's the answer!" he said. "The damn grafters!"

Miss Jackson came in again.

"Mr. Robert Blair is waiting to see you."

"Who is he?"

"You know. He tried to write some things for one of the shows last year."

"Oh, yes. Say, did you send flowers to Plant's house?"

"I did," replied Miss Jackson. "I sent some beautiful roses."

"How much?"

"Forty-five dollars," said Miss Jackson.

"Forty-five dollars for roses! And the man hated flowers even when he was alive! Well, send in this Blair."

Robert Blair was an ambitious young free lance who had long been trying to write for the stage, but with little success.

"Sit down, Blair," said Green. "What's on your mind?"

"Well, Mr. Green, my stuff didn't seem to suit you last year, but this time I think I've got a scene that can't miss."

"All right. If you want to leave it here, I'll read it over."

"I haven't written it out. I thought I'd tell you the idea first."

"Well, go ahead, but cut it short; I've got a lot of things to do today. Got to go to old Plant's funeral for one thing."

"I bet you miss him, don't you?" said Blair, sympathetically.

"Miss him! I should say I do! A lovable character and"—with a glance at Lewis—"the best secretary I'll ever have. But let's hear your scene."

"Well," said Blair, "it may not sound like much the way I tell it, but I think it'll work out great. Well, the police get a report that a woman has been murdered in her home, and they go there and find her husband, who is acting very nervous. They give him the third degree, and he finally breaks down and admits he killed her. They ask him why, and he tells them he is very fond of beans, and on the preceding evening he came home to dinner and asked her what there was to eat, and she told him she had lamb chops, mashed potatoes, spinach, and apple pie. So he says, 'No beans?' and she says, 'No beans.' So he shoots her dead. Of course, the scene between the husband and wife is acted out on the stage. Then——"

"It's no good!" said Conrad Green. "In the first place, it takes too many people, all those policemen and everybody."

"Why, all you need is two policemen and the man and his wife. And wait till I tell you the rest of it."

"I don't like it; it's no good. Come back again when you've got something."

When Blair had gone Green turned to Lewis.

"That's all for just now," he said, "but on your way out tell Miss Jackson to get a hold of Martin and say I want him to drop in here as soon as he can."

"What Martin?" asked Lewis.

"She'll know—Joe Martin, the man that writes most of our librettos."

Alone, Conrad Green crossed the room to his safe, opened it, and took out a box on which was inscribed the name of a Philadelphia jeweler. From the box he removed a beautiful rope of matched pearls and was gazing at them in admiration when Miss Jackson came in; whereupon he hastily replaced them in their case and closed the safe.

"That man is here again," said Miss Jackson, "That man Hawley from *Gay New York*."

"Tell him I'm not in."

"I did, but he says he saw you come in and he's going to wait till you'll talk to him. Really, Mr. Green, I think it would be best in the long run to see him. He's awfully persistent."

"All right; send him in," said Green, impatiently, "though I have no idea what he can possibly want of me."

Mr. Hawley, dapper and eternally smiling, insisted on shaking hands with his unwilling host, who had again sat down at his desk.

"I think," he said, "we've met before."

"Not that I know of," Green replied shortly.

"Well, it makes no difference, but I'm sure you've read our little paper, *Gay New York*."

"No," said Green. "All I have time to read is manuscripts."

"You don't know what you're missing," said Hawley. "It's really a growing paper, with a big New York circulation, and a circulation that is important from your standpoint."

"Are you soliciting subscriptions?" asked Green.

"No. Advertising."

"Well, frankly, Mr. Hawley, I don't believe I need any advertising. I believe that even the advertising I put in the regular daily papers is a waste of money."

"Just the same," said Hawley, "I think you'd be making a mistake not to take a page in *Gay New York*. It's only a matter of fifteen hundred dollars."

"Fifteen hundred dollars! That's a joke! Nobody's going to hold *me* up!"

"Nobody's trying to, Mr. Green. But I might as well tell you that one of our reporters came in with a story the other day— well, it was about a little gambling affair in which some of the losers sort of forgot to settle, and—well, my partner was all for printing it, but I said I had always felt friendly toward you and why not give you a chance to state your side of it?"

"I don't know what you're talking about. If your reporter has got my name mixed up in a gambling story he's crazy."

"No. He's perfectly sane and very, very careful. We make a specialty of careful reporters and we're always sure of our facts."

Conrad Green was silent for a long, long time. Then he said:

"I tell you, I don't know what gambling business you refer to, and, furthermore, fifteen hundred dollars is a hell of a price for a page in a paper like yours. But still, as you say, you've got the kind of circulation that might do me good. So if you'll cut down the price——"

"I'm sorry, Mr. Green, but we never do that."

"Well, then, of course you'll have to give me a few days to get my ad fixed up. Say you come back here next Monday afternoon."

"That's perfectly satisfactory, Mr. Green," said Hawley, "and I assure you that you're not making a mistake. And now I won't keep you any longer from your work."

He extended his hand, but it was ignored, and he went out, his smile a little broader than when he had come in. Green remained at his desk, staring straight ahead of him and making semi-audible references to certain kinds of dogs as well as personages referred to in the Old and New Testaments. He was interrupted by the entrance of Lewis.

"Mr. Green," said the new secretary, "I have found a check for forty-five dollars made out to Herman Plant. I imagine it is for his final week's pay. Would you like to have me change it and make it out to his widow?"

"Yes," said Green. "But no; wait a minute. Tear it up and I'll make out my personal check to her and add something to it."

"All right," said Lewis, and left.

"Forty-five dollars' worth of flowers," said Green to himself, and smiled for the first time that morning.

He looked at his watch and got up and put on his beautiful hat.

"I'm going to lunch," he told Miss Jackson on his way through the outer office. "If Peebles or anybody important calls up, tell them I'll be here all afternoon."

"You're not forgetting Mr. Plant's funeral?"

"Oh, that's right. Well, I'll be here from one-thirty to about three."

A head waiter at the Astor bowed to him obsequiously and escorted him to a table near a window, while the occupants of several other tables gazed at him spellbound and whispered, "Conrad Green."

A luncheon of clams, sweetbreads, spinach, strawberry ice cream, and small coffee seemed to satisfy him. He signed his check and then tipped his own waiter and the head waiter a dollar apiece, the two tips falling just short of the cost of the meal.

Joe Martin, his chief librettist, was waiting when he got back to his office.

"Oh, hello, Joe!" he said, cordially. "Come right inside. I think I've got something for you."

Martin followed him in and sat down without waiting for an invitation. Green seated himself at his desk and drew out his cigarette case.

"Have one, Joe?"

"Not that kind!" said Martin, lighting one of his own. "You've gotten rotten taste in everything but gals."

"And librettists," replied Green, smiling.

"But here's what I wanted to talk about. I couldn't sleep last night, and I just laid there and an idea came to me for a comedy scene. I'll give you the bare idea and you can work it out. It'll take a girl and one of the comics, maybe Fraser, and a couple of other men that can play.

"Well, the idea is that the comic is married to the girl. In the first place, I'd better mention that the comic is crazy about beans. Well, one night the comic—no, wait a minute. The police get word that the comic's wife has been murdered and two policemen come to the comic's apartment to investigate. They examine the corpse and find out she's been shot through the head. They ask the comic if he knows who did it and he says no, but they keep after him, and finally he breaks down and admits that he did it himself.

"But he says, 'Gentlemen, if you'll let me explain the circumstances, I don't believe you'll arrest me.' So they tell him to explain, and he says that he came home from work and he was very hungry and he asked his wife what they were going to have for dinner. So she tells him—clams and sweetbreads and spinach and strawberry ice cream and coffee. So he asks her if she isn't going to have any beans and she says no, and he shoots her. What do you think you could do with that idea?"

"Listen, Connie," said Martin: "You've only got half the scene, and you've got that half wrong. In the second place, it was played a whole season in the Music Box and it was written by Bert Kalmar and Harry Ruby. Otherwise I can do a whole lot with it."

"Are you sure you're right?"

"I certainly am!"

"Why, that damn little thief! He told me it was his!"

"Who?" asked Martin.

"Why, that Blair, that tried to butt in here last year. I'll fix him!"

"I thought you said it was your own idea."

"Hell, no! Do you think I'd be stealing stuff, especially if it was a year old?"

"Well," said Martin, "when you get another inspiration like this, give me a ring and I'll come around. Now I've got to hurry up to the old Stadium and see what the old Babe does in the first inning."

"I'm sorry, Joe. I thought it was perfectly all right."

"Never mind! You didn't waste much of my time. But after this you'd better leave the ideas to me. So long!"

"Good-by, Joe; and thanks for coming in."

Martin went and Green pressed the button for Miss Jackson.

"Miss Jackson, don't ever let that young Blair in here again. He's a faker!"

"All right, Mr. Green. But don't you think it's about time you were starting for the funeral? It's twenty minutes of three."

"Yes. But let's see: where is Plant's house?"

"It's up on One Hundred and Sixtieth street, just off Broadway."

"My God! Imagine living there! Wait a minute, Miss Jackson. Send Lewis here."

"Lewis," he said, when the new secretary appeared, "I ate something this noon that disagreed with me. I wanted to go up to Plant's funeral, but I really think it would be dangerous to try it. Will you go up there, let them know who you are, and kind of represent me? Miss Jackson will give you the address."

"Yes, sir," said Lewis, and went out.

Almost immediately the sanctum door opened again and the beautiful Marjorie Green, née Manning, entered unannounced. Green's face registered not altogether pleasant surprise.

"Why, hello, dear!" he said. "I didn't know you were coming to town today."

"I never told you I wasn't," his wife replied.

They exchanged the usual connubial salutations.

"I supposed you noticed," said Mrs. Green, "that our names were not on the list of guests at the party."

"No; I haven't had time to look at the papers. But what's the difference?"

"No difference at all, of course. But do you know what I think? I think we were invited just because those people want to get something out of you, for some benefit or something."

"A fine chance! I hope they try it!"

"However, that's not what I came to talk about."

"Well, dear, what is it?"

"I thought maybe you'd remember something."

"What, honey?"

"Why—oh, well, there's no use talking about it if you've forgotten."

Green's forehead wrinkled in deep thought; then suddenly his face brightened.

"Of course I haven't forgotten! It's your birthday!"

"You just thought of it now!"

"No such a thing! I've been thinking of it for weeks!"

"I don't believe you! If you had been, you'd have said something, and"—his wife was on the verge of tears—"you'd have given me some little thing, just any little thing."

Once more Green frowned, and once more brightened up.

"I'll prove it to you," he said, and walked rapidly to the safe.

In a moment he had placed in her hands the jewel box from Philadelphia. In another moment she had opened it, gasped at the beauty of its contents, and thrown her arms around his neck.

"Oh, dearest!" she cried. "Can you ever forgive me for doubting you?"

She put the pearls to her mouth as if she would eat them.

"But haven't you been terribly extravagant?"

"I don't consider anything too extravagant for you."

"You're the best husband a girl ever had!"

"I'm glad you're pleased," said Green.

"Pleased! I'm overwhelmed. And to think I imagined you'd

forgotten! But I'm not going to break up your whole day. I know you want to get out to poor old Plant's funeral. So I'll run along. And maybe you'll take me to dinner somewhere to-night."

"I certainly will! You be at the Ambassador about six-thirty and we'll have a little birthday party. But don't you want to leave the pearls here now?"

"I should say not! They're going to stay with me forever! Anyone that tries to take them will do it over my dead body!"

"Well, good-by, then, dear."

"Till half past six."

Green, alone again, kicked shut the door of his safe and re-turned to his desk, saying in loud tones things which are not ordinarily considered appropriate to the birthday of a loved one. The hubbub must have been audible to Miss Jackson outside, but perhaps she was accustomed to it. It ceased at another unan-nounced entrance, that of a girl even more beautiful than the one who had just gone out. She looked at Green and laughed.

"My God! You look happy!" she said.

"Rose!"

"Yes, it's Rose. But what's the matter with you?"

"I've had a bad day."

"But isn't it better now?"

"I didn't think you were coming till to-morrow."

"But aren't you glad I came today?"

"You bet I am!" said Green. "And if you'll come here and kiss me I'll be all the gladder."

"No. Let's get our business transacted first."

"What business?"

"You know perfectly well! Last time I saw you you insisted that I must give up everybody else but you. And I promised you it would be all off between Harry and I if—— Well, you know. There was a little matter of some pearls."

"I meant everything I said."

"Well, where are they?"

"They're all bought and all ready for you. But I bought them in Philadelphia and for some damned reason they haven't got here yet."

"Got here yet! Were they so heavy you couldn't bring them with you?"

"Honest, dear, they'll be here day after tomorrow at the latest."

" 'Honest' is a good word for you to use! Do you think I'm dumb? Or is it that you're so used to lying that you can't help it?"

"If you'll let me explain——"

"Explain hell! We made a bargain and you haven't kept your end of it. And now——"

"But listen——"

"I'll listen to nothing! You know where to reach me and when you've kept your promise you can call me up. Till then— Well, Harry isn't such bad company."

"Wait a minute, Rose!"

"You've heard all I've got to say. Good-by!"

And she was gone before he could intercept her.

Conrad Green sat as if stunned. For fifteen minutes he was so silent and motionless that one might have thought him dead. Then he shivered as if with cold and said aloud:

"I'm not going to worry about them any more. To hell with all of them!"

He drew the telephone to him and took off the receiver.

"Get me Mrs. Bryant-Walker."

And after a pause:

"Is this Mrs. Bryant-Walker? No, I want to speak to her personally. This is Conrad Green. Oh, hello, Mrs. Walker. Your secretary called me up this morning, but we were cut off. She was saying something about a benefit. Why, yes, certainly, I'll be glad to. As many of them as you want. If you'll just leave it all in my hands I'll guarantee you a pretty good entertainment. It's no bother at all. It's a pleasure. Thank you. Good-by."

Lewis came in.

"Well, Lewis, did you get to the funeral?"

"Yes, Mr. Green, and I saw Mrs. Plant and explained the circumstances to her. She said you had always been very kind to her husband. She said that during the week of his illness he talked of you nearly all the time and expressed confidence that if he died you would attend his funeral. So she wished you had been there."

"Good God! So do I!" said Conrad Green.

THE LOVE NEST

"I'll tell you what I'm going to do with you, Mr. Bartlett," said the great man. "I'm going to take you right out to my home and have you meet the wife and family; stay to dinner and all night. We've got plenty of room and extra pajamas, if you don't mind them silk. I mean that'll give you a chance to see us just as we are. I mean you can get more that way than if you sat here a whole week, asking me questions."

"But I don't want to put you to a lot of trouble," said Bartlett.

"Trouble!" The great man laughed. "There's no trouble about it. I've got a house that's like a hotel. I mean a big house with lots of servants. But anyway I'm always glad to do anything I can for a writing man, especially a man that works for Ralph Doane. I'm very fond of Ralph. I mean I like him personally besides being a great editor. I mean I've known him for years and when there's anything I can do for him, I'm glad to do it. I mean it'll be a pleasure to have you. So if you want to notify your family——"

"I haven't any family," said Bartlett.

"Well, I'm sorry for you! And I bet when you see mine, you'll wish you had one of your own. But I'm glad you can come and we'll start now so as to get there before the kiddies are put away for the night. I mean I want you to be sure and see the kiddies. I've got three."

"I've seen their pictures," said Bartlett. "You must be very proud of them. They're all girls, aren't they?"

"Yes, sir; three girls. I wouldn't have a boy. I mean I always
wanted girls. I mean girls have got a lot more zip to them. I mean
they're a lot zippier. But let's go! The Rolls is downstairs and if
we start now we'll get there before dark. I mean I want you
to see the place while it's still daylight."

The great man—Lou Gregg, president of Modern Pictures,
Inc.—escorted his visitor from the magnificent office by a private door and down a private stairway to the avenue, where the
glittering car with its glittering chauffeur waited.

"My wife was in town today," said Gregg as they glided
northward, "and I hoped we could ride out together, but she
called up about two and asked would I mind if she went on
home in the Pierce. She was through with her shopping and
she hates to be away from the house and the kiddies any longer
than she can help. Celia's a great home girl. You'd never know
she was the same girl now as the girl I married seven years ago. I
mean she's different. I mean she's not the same. I mean her marriage and being a mother has developed her. Did you ever see
her? I mean in pictures?"

"I think I did once," replied Bartlett. "Didn't she play the
young sister in 'The Cad'?"

"Yes, with Harold Hodgson and Marie Blythe."

"I thought I'd seen her. I remember her as very pretty and
vivacious."

"She certainly was! And she is yet! I mean she's even prettier,
but of course she ain't a kid, though she looks it. I mean she was
only seventeen in that picture and that was ten years ago. I
mean she's twenty-seven years old now. But I never met a girl
with as much zip as she had in those days. It's remarkable how
marriage changes them. I mean nobody would ever thought
Celia Sayles would turn out to be a sit-by-the-fire. I mean she still
likes a good time, but her home and kiddies come first. I mean
her home and kiddies come first."

"I see what you mean," said Bartlett.

An hour's drive brought them to Ardsley-on-Hudson and the great man's home.

"A wonderful place!" Bartlett exclaimed with a heroic semblance of enthusiasm as the car turned in at an *arc de triomphe* of a gateway and approached a white house that might have been mistaken for the Yale Bowl.

"It ought to be!" said Gregg. "I mean I've spent enough on it. I mean these things cost money."

He indicated with a gesture the huge house and Urbanesque landscaping.

"But no amount of money is too much to spend on home. I mean it's a good investment if it tends to make your family proud and satisfied with their home. I mean every nickel I've spent here is like so much insurance; it insures me of a happy wife and family. And what more can a man ask!"

Bartlett didn't know, but the topic was forgotten in the business of leaving the resplendent Rolls and entering the even more resplendent reception hall.

"Forbes will take your things," said Gregg. "And, Forbes, you may tell Dennis that Mr. Bartlett will spend the night." He faced the wide stairway and raised his voice. "Sweetheart!" he called.

From above came the reply in contralto: "Hello, sweetheart!"

"Come down, sweetheart. I've brought you a visitor."

"All right, sweetheart, in just a minute."

Gregg led Bartlett into a living-room that was five laps to the mile and suggestive of an Atlantic City auction sale.

"Sit there," said the host, pointing to a balloon-stuffed easy chair, "and I'll see if we can get a drink. I've got some real old Bourbon that I'd like you to try. You know I come from Chicago and I always liked Bourbon better than Scotch. I mean I always preferred it to Scotch. Forbes," he addressed the servant, "we want a drink. You'll find a full bottle of that Bourbon in the cupboard."

"It's only half full, sir," said Forbes.

"Half full! That's funny! I mean I opened it last night and just took one drink. I mean it ought to be full."

"It's only half full," repeated Forbes, and went to fetch it.

"I'll have to investigate," Gregg told his guest. "I mean this ain't the first time lately that some of my good stuff has disappeared. When you keep so many servants, it's hard to get all honest ones. But here's Celia!"

Bartlett rose to greet the striking brunette who at this moment made an entrance so Delsarte as to be almost painful. With never a glance at him, she minced across the room to her husband and took a half interest in a convincing kiss.

"Well, sweetheart," she said when it was at last over.

"This is Mr. Bartlett, sweetheart," said her husband. "Mr. Bartlett, meet Mrs. Gregg."

Bartlett shook his hostess's proffered two fingers.

"I'm so pleased!" said Celia in a voice reminiscent of Miss Claire's imitation of Miss Barrymore.

"Mr. Bartlett," Gregg went on, "is with *Mankind*, Ralph Doane's magazine. He is going to write me up; I mean us."

"No, you mean you," said Celia. "I'm sure the public is not interested in great men's wives."

"I am sure you are mistaken, Mrs. Gregg," said Bartlett politely. "In this case at least. You are worth writing up aside from being a great man's wife."

"I'm afraid you're a flatterer, Mr. Bartlett," she returned. "I have been out of the limelight so long that I doubt if anybody remembers me. I'm no longer an artist; merely a happy wife and mother."

"And I claim, sweetheart," said Gregg, "that it takes an artist to be that."

"Oh, no, sweetheart!" said Celia. "Not when they have you for a husband!"

The exchange of hosannahs was interrupted by the arrival of Forbes with the tray.

"Will you take yours straight or in a high-ball?" Gregg inquired of his guest. "Personally I like good whisky straight. I mean mixing it with water spoils the flavor. I mean whisky like this, it seems like a crime to mix it with water."

"I'll have mine straight," said Bartlett, who would have preferred a high-ball.

While the drinks were being prepared, he observed his hostess more closely and thought how much more charming she would be if she had used finesse in improving on nature. Her cheeks, her mouth, her eyes, and lashes had been, he guessed, far above the average in beauty before she had begun experimenting with them. And her experiments had been clumsy. She was handsome in spite of her efforts to be handsomer.

"Listen, sweetheart," said her husband. "One of the servants has been helping himself to this Bourbon. I mean it was a full bottle last night and I only had one little drink out of it. And now it's less than half full. Who do you suppose has been at it?"

"How do I know, sweetheart? Maybe the groceryman or the iceman or somebody."

"But you and I and Forbes are the only ones that have a key. I mean it was locked up."

"Maybe you forgot to lock it."

"I never do. Well, anyway, Bartlett, here's a go!"

"Doesn't Mrs. Gregg indulge?" asked Bartlett.

"Only a cocktail before dinner," said Celia. "Lou objects to me drinking whisky, and I don't like it much anyway."

"I don't object to you drinking whisky, sweetheart. I just object to you drinking to excess. I mean I think it coarsens a woman to drink. I mean it makes them coarse."

"Well, there's no argument, sweetheart. As I say, I don't care whether I have it or not."

"It certainly is great Bourbon!" said Bartlett, smacking his lips and putting his glass back on the tray.

"You bet it is!" Gregg agreed. "I mean you can't buy that kind of stuff any more. I mean it's real stuff. You help yourself when you want another. Mr. Bartlett is going to stay all night, sweetheart. I told him he could get a whole lot more of a line on us that way than just interviewing me in the office. I mean I'm tongue-tied when it comes to talking about my work and my success. I mean it's better to see me out here as I am, in my home, with my family. I mean my home life speaks for itself without me saying a word."

"But, sweetheart," said his wife, "what about Mr. Latham?"

"Gosh! I forgot all about him! I must phone and see if I can call it off. That's terrible! You see," he explained to Bartlett, "I made a date to go up to Tarrytown tonight, to K. L. Latham's, the sugar people. We're going to talk over the new club. We're going to have a golf club that will make the rest of them look like a toy. I mean a real golf club! They want me to kind of run it. And I was to go up there tonight and talk it over. I'll phone and see if I can postpone it."

"Oh, don't postpone it on my account!" urged Bartlett. "I can come out again some other time, or I can see you in town."

"I don't see how you *can* postpone it, sweetheart," said Celia. "Didn't he say old Mr. King was coming over from White Plains? They'll be mad at you if you don't go."

"I'm afraid they would resent it, sweetheart. Well, I'll tell you. You can entertain Mr. Bartlett and I'll go there right after dinner and come back as soon as I can. And Bartlett and I can talk when I get back. I mean we can talk when I get back. How is that?"

"That suits me," said Bartlett.

"I'll be as entertaining as I can," said Celia, "but I'm afraid that isn't very entertaining. However, if I'm too much of a bore, there's plenty to read."

"No danger of my being bored," said Bartlett.

"Well, that's all fixed then," said the relieved host. "I hope you'll excuse me running away. But I don't see how I can get out of it. I mean with old King coming over from White Plains. I mean he's an old man. But listen, sweetheart—where are the kiddies? Mr. Bartlett wants to see them."

"Yes, indeed!" agreed the visitor.

"Of course you'd say so!" Celia said. "But we *are* proud of them! I suppose all parents are the same. They all think their own children are the only children in the world. Isn't that so, Mr. Bartlett? Or haven't you any children?"

"I'm sorry to say I'm not married."

"Oh, you poor thing! We pity him, don't we, sweetheart? But why aren't you, Mr. Bartlett? Don't tell me you're a woman hater!"

"Not now, anyway," said the gallant Bartlett.

"Do you get that, sweetheart? He's paying you a pretty compliment."

"I heard it, sweetheart. And now I'm sure he's a flatterer. But I must hurry and get the children before Hortense puts them to bed."

"Well," said Gregg when his wife had left the room, "would you say she's changed?"

"A little, and for the better. She's more than fulfilled her early promise."

"I think so," said Gregg. "I mean I think she was a beautiful girl and now she's an even more beautiful woman. I mean wifehood and maternity have given her a kind of a—well, you know —I mean a kind of a pose. I mean a pose. How about another drink?"

They were emptying their glasses when Celia returned with two of her little girls.

"The baby's in bed and I was afraid to ask Hortense to get her up again. But you'll see her in the morning. This is Norma and this is Grace. Girls, this is Mr. Bartlett."

The girls received this news calmly.

"Well, girls," said Bartlett.

"What do you think of them, Bartlett?" demanded their father. "I mean what do you think of them?"

"They're great!" replied the guest with creditable warmth.

"I mean aren't they pretty?"

"I should say they are!"

"There, girls! Why don't you thank Mr. Bartlett?"

"Thanks," murmured Norma.

"How old are you, Norma?" asked Bartlett.

"Six," said Norma.

"Well," said Bartlett. "And how old is Grace?"

"Four," replied Norma.

"Well," said Bartlett. "And how old is baby sister?"

"One and a half," answered Norma.

"Well," said Bartlett.

As this seemed to be final, "Come, girls," said their mother. "Kiss daddy good night and I'll take you back to Hortense."

"I'll take them," said Gregg. "I'm going up-stairs anyway. And you can show Bartlett around. I mean before it gets any darker."

"Good night, girls," said Bartlett, and the children murmured a good night.

"I'll come and see you before you're asleep," Celia told them. And after Gregg had led them out, "Do you really think they're pretty?" she asked Bartlett.

"I certainly do. Especially Norma. She's the image of you," said Bartlett.

"She looks a little like I used to," Celia admitted. "But I hope she doesn't look like me now. I'm too old looking."

"You look remarkably young!" said Bartlett. "No one would believe you were the mother of three children."

"Oh, Mr. Bartlett! But I mustn't forget I'm to 'show you around.' Lou is so proud of our home!"

"And with reason," said Bartlett.

"It *is* wonderful! I call it our love nest. Quite a big nest, don't you think? Mother says it's too big to be cosy; she says she can't think of it as a home. But I always say a place is whatever one makes of it. A woman can be happy in a tent if they love each other. And miserable in a royal palace without love. Don't you think so, Mr. Bartlett?"

"Yes, indeed."

"Is this really such wonderful Bourbon? I think I'll just take a sip of it and see what it's like. It can't hurt me if it's so good. Do you think so, Mr. Bartlett?"

"I don't believe so."

"Well then, I'm going to taste it and if it hurts me it's your fault."

Celia poured a whisky glass two-thirds full and drained it at a gulp.

"It *is* good, isn't it?" she said. "Of course I'm not much of a judge as I don't care for whisky and Lou won't let me drink it. But he's raved so about this Bourbon that I did want to see what it was like. You won't tell on me, will you, Mr. Bartlett?"

"Not I!"

"I wonder how it would be in a high-ball. Let's you and I have just one. But I'm forgetting I'm supposed to show you the place. We won't have time to drink a high-ball and see the place too before Lou comes down. Are you so crazy to see the place?"

"Not very."

"Well, then, what do you say if we have a high-ball? And it'll be a secret between you and I."

They drank in silence and Celia pressed a button by the door.

"You may take the bottle and tray," she told Forbes. "And now," she said to Bartlett, "we'll go out on the porch and see as much as we can see. You'll have to guess the rest."

Gregg, having changed his shirt and collar, joined them. "Well," he said to Bartlett, "have you seen everything?"

"I guess I have, Mr. Gregg," lied the guest readily. "It's a wonderful place!"

"We like it. I mean it suits us. I mean it's my idear of a real home. And Celia calls it her love nest."

"So she told me," said Bartlett.

"She'll always be sentimental," said her husband.

He put his hand on her shoulder, but she drew away.

"I must run up and dress," she said.

"Dress!" exclaimed Bartlett, who had been dazzled by her flowered green chiffon.

"Oh, I'm not going to really dress," she said. "But I couldn't wear this thing for dinner!"

"Perhaps you'd like to clean up a little, Bartlett," said Gregg. "I mean Forbes will show you your room if you want to go up."

"It might be best," said Bartlett.

Celia, in a black lace dinner gown, was rather quiet during the elaborate meal. Three or four times when Gregg addressed her, she seemed to be thinking of something else and had to ask, "What did you say, sweetheart?" Her face was red and Bartlett imagined that she had "sneaked" a drink or two besides the two helpings of Bourbon and the cocktail that had preceded dinner.

"Well, I'll leave you," said Gregg when they were in the living-room once more. "I mean the sooner I get started, the sooner I'll be back. Sweetheart, try and keep your guest awake and don't let him die of thirst. *Au revoir*, Bartlett. I'm sorry, but it can't be helped. There's a fresh bottle of the Bourbon, so go to it. I mean help yourself. It's too bad you have to drink alone."

"It *is* too bad, Mr. Bartlett," said Celia when Gregg had gone.

"What's too bad?" asked Bartlett.

"That you have to drink alone. I feel like I wasn't being a good hostess to let you do it. In fact, I refuse to let you do it. I'll join you in just a little wee sip."

"But it's so soon after dinner!"

"It's never too soon! I'm going to have a drink myself and if you don't join me, you're a quitter."

She mixed two life-sized high-balls and handed one to her guest.

"Now we'll turn on the radio and see if we can't stir things up. There! No, no! Who cares about the old baseball! Now! This is better! Let's dance."

"I'm sorry, Mrs. Gregg, but I don't dance."

"Well, you're an old cheese. To make me dance alone! 'All alone, yes, I'm all alone.' "

There was no affectation in her voice now and Bartlett was amazed at her unlabored grace as she glided around the big room.

"But it's no fun alone," she complained. "Let's shut the damn thing off and talk."

"I love to watch you dance," said Bartlett.

"Yes, but I'm no Pavlowa," said Celia as she silenced the radio. "And besides, it's time for a drink."

"I've still got more than half of mine."

"Well, you had that wine at dinner, so I'll have to catch up with you."

She poured herself another high-ball and went at the task of "catching up."

"The trouble with you, Mr.—now isn't that a scream! I can't think of your name."

"Bartlett."

"The trouble with you, Barker—do you know what's the trouble with you? You're too sober. See? You're too damn sober! That's the whole trouble, see? If you weren't so sober, we'd be better off. See? What I can't understand is how you can be so sober and me so high."

"You're not used to it."

"Not used to it! That's the cat's pajamas! Say, I'm like this half the time, see? If I wasn't, I'd die!"

"What does your husband say?"

"He don't say because he don't know. See, Barker? There's nights when he's out and there's a few nights when I'm out myself. And there's other nights when we're both in and I pretend I'm sleepy and I go up-stairs. See? But I don't go to bed. See? I have a little party all by myself. See? If I didn't, I'd die!"

"What do you mean, you'd die?"

"You're dumb, Barker! You may be sober, but you're dumb! Did you fall for all that apple sauce about the happy home and the contented wife? Listen, Barker—I'd give anything in the world to be out of this mess. I'd give anything to never see him again."

"Don't you love him any more? Doesn't he love you? Or what?"

"Love! I never did love him! I didn't know what love was! And all his love is for himself!"

"How did you happen to get married?"

"I was a kid; that's the answer. A kid and ambitious. See? He was a director then and he got stuck on me and I thought he'd make me a star. See, Barker? I married him to get myself a chance. And now look at me!"

"I'd say you were fairly well off."

"Well off, am I? I'd change places with the scum of the earth just to be free! See, Barker? And I could have been a star without any help if I'd only realized it. I had the looks and I had the talent. I've got it yet. I could be a Swanson and get myself a marquis; maybe a prince! And look what I did get! A self-satisfied, self-centered——! I thought he'd *make* me! See, Barker? Well, he's made me all right; he's made me a chronic mother and it's a wonder I've got any looks left.

"I fought at first. I told him marriage didn't mean giving up my art, my life work. But it was no use. He wanted a beautiful wife and beautiful children for his beautiful home. Just to show us off. See? I'm part of his chattels. See, Barker? I'm just like his big diamond or his cars or his horses. And he wouldn't stand for his wife 'lowering' herself to act in pictures. Just as if pictures hadn't made him!

"You go back to your magazine tomorrow and write about our love nest. See, Barker? And be sure and don't get mixed and call it a baby ranch. Babies! You thought little Norma was pretty. Well, she is. And what is it going to get her? A rich —— of a husband that treats her like a ——! That's what it'll get her if I don't interfere. I hope I don't last long enough to see her grow up, but if I do, I'm going to advise her to run away from home and live her own life. And *be* somebody! Not a *thing* like I am! See, Barker?"

"Did you ever think of a divorce?"

"Did I ever think of one! Listen—but there's no chance. I've got nothing on him, and no matter what he had on me, he'd never let the world know it. He'd keep me here and torture me like he does now, only worse. But I haven't done anything wrong, see? The men I might care for, they're all scared of him and his money and power. See, Barker? And the others are just as bad as him. Like fat old Morris, the hotel man, that everybody thinks he's a model husband. The reason he don't step out more is because he's too stingy. But I could have him if I wanted him. Every time he gets near enough to me, he squeezes my hand. I guess he thinks it's a nickel, the tight old ——! But come on, Barker. Let's have a drink. I'm running down."

"I think it's about time you were running up—up-stairs," said Bartlett. "If I were you, I'd try to be in bed and asleep when Gregg gets home."

"You're all right, Barker. And after this drink I'm going to do just as you say. Only I thought of it before you did, see? I think of it lots of nights. And tonight you can help me out by telling him I had a bad headache."

Left alone, Bartlett thought a while, then read, and finally dozed off. He was dozing when Gregg returned.

"Well, well, Bartlett," said the great man, "did Celia desert you?"

"It was perfectly all right, Mr. Gregg. She had a headache and I told her to go to bed."

"She's had a lot of headaches lately; reads too much, I guess. Well, I'm sorry I had this date. It was about a new golf club and I had to be there. I mean I'm going to be president of it. I see you consoled yourself with some of the Bourbon. I mean the bottle doesn't look as full as it did."

"I hope you'll forgive me for helping myself so generously," said Bartlett. "I don't get stuff like that every day!"

"Well, what do you say if we turn in? We can talk on the way to town tomorrow. Though I guess you won't have much to ask me. I guess you know all about us. I mean you know all about us now."

"Yes, indeed, Mr. Gregg. I've got plenty of material if I can just handle it."

Celia had not put in an appearance when Gregg and his guest were ready to leave the house next day.

"She always sleeps late," said Gregg. "I mean she never wakes up very early. But she's later than usual this morning. Sweetheart!" he called up the stairs.

"Yes, sweetheart," came the reply.

"Mr. Bartlett's leaving now. I mean he's going."

"Oh, good-by, Mr. Bartlett. Please forgive me for not being down to see you off."

"You're forgiven, Mrs. Gregg. And thanks for your hospitality."

"Good-by, sweetheart!"

"Good-by, sweetheart!"

THE GOLDEN HONEYMOON

Mother says that when I start talking I never know when to stop. But I tell her the only time I get a chance is when she ain't around, so I have to make the most of it. I guess the fact is neither one of us would be welcome in a Quaker meeting, but as I tell Mother, what did God give us tongues for if He didn't want we should use them? Only she says He didn't give them to us to say the same thing over and over again, like I do, and repeat myself. But I say:

"Well, Mother," I say, "when people is like you and I and been married fifty years, do you expect everything I say will be something you ain't heard me say before? But it may be new to others, as they ain't nobody else lived with me as long as you have."

So she says:

"You can bet they ain't, as they couldn't nobody else stand you that long."

"Well," I tell her, "you look pretty healthy."

"Maybe I do," she will say, "but I looked even healthier before I married you."

You can't get ahead of Mother.

Yes, sir, we was married just fifty years ago the seventeenth day of last December and my daughter and son-in-law was over from Trenton to help us celebrate the Golden Wedding. My son-in-law is John H. Kramer, the real estate man. He made

$12,000 one year and is pretty well thought of around Trenton; a good, steady, hard worker. The Rotarians was after him a long time to join, but he kept telling them his home was his club. But Edie finally made him join. That's my daughter.

Well, anyway, they come over to help us celebrate the Golden Wedding and it was pretty crimpy weather and the furnace don't seem to heat up no more like it used to and Mother made the remark that she hoped this winter wouldn't be as cold as the last, referring to the winter previous. So Edie said if she was us, and nothing to keep us home, she certainly wouldn't spend no more winters up here and why didn't we just shut off the water and close up the house and go down to Tampa, Florida? You know we was there four winters ago and staid five weeks, but it cost us over three hundred and fifty dollars for hotel bill alone. So Mother said we wasn't going no place to be robbed. So my son-in-law spoke up and said that Tampa wasn't the only place in the South, and besides we didn't have to stop at no high price hotel but could rent us a couple of rooms and board out somewheres, and he had heard that St. Petersburg, Florida, was *the* spot and if we said the word he would write down there and make inquiries.

Well, to make a long story short, we decided to do it and Edie said it would be our Golden Honeymoon and for a present my son-in-law paid the difference between a section and a compartment so as we could have a compartment and have more privatecy. In a compartment you have an upper and lower berth just like the regular sleeper, but it is a shut in room by itself and got a wash bowl. The car we went in was all compartments and no regular berths at all. It was all compartments.

We went to Trenton the night before and staid at my daughter and son-in-law and we left Trenton the next afternoon at 3.23 P.M.

This was the twelfth day of January. Mother set facing the front of the train, as it makes her giddy to ride backwards. I set

facing her, which does not affect me. We reached North Philadelphia at 4.03 P.M. and we reached West Philadelphia at 4.14,
but did not go into Broad Street. We reached Baltimore at 6.30
and Washington, D.C., at 7.25. Our train laid over in Washington two hours till another train come along to pick us up and I
got out and strolled up the platform and into the Union Station.
When I come back, our car had been switched on to another
track, but I remembered the name of it, the La Belle, as I had
once visited my aunt out in Oconomowoc, Wisconsin, where
there was a lake of that name, so I had no difficulty in getting
located. But Mother had nearly fretted herself sick for fear I
would be left.

"Well," I said, "I would of followed you on the next train."

"You could of," said Mother, and she pointed out that she had
the money.

"Well," I said, "we are in Washington and I could of borrowed
from the United States Treasury. I would of pretended I was an
Englishman."

Mother caught the point and laughed heartily.

Our train pulled out of Washington at 9.40 P.M. and Mother
and I turned in early, I taking the upper. During the night we
passed through the green fields of old Virginia, though it was
too dark to tell if they was green or what color. When we got up
in the morning, we was at Fayetteville, North Carolina. We had
breakfast in the dining car and after breakfast I got in conversation with the man in the next compartment to ours. He was from
Lebanon, New Hampshire, and a man about eighty years of age.
His wife was with him, and two unmarried daughters and I made
the remark that I should think the four of them would be crowded
in one compartment, but he said they had made the trip every
winter for fifteen years and knowed how to keep out of each
other's way. He said they was bound for Tarpon Springs.

We reached Charleston, South Carolina, at 12.50 P.M. and arrived at Savannah, Georgia, at 4.20. We reached Jacksonville,

Florida, at 8.45 P.M. and had an hour and a quarter to lay over there, but Mother made a fuss about me getting off the train, so we had the darky make up our berths and retired before we left Jacksonville. I didn't sleep good as the train done a lot of hemming and hawing, and Mother never sleeps good on a train as she says she is always worrying that I will fall out. She says she would rather have the upper herself, as then she would not have to worry about me, but I tell her I can't take the risk of having it get out that I allowed my wife to sleep in an upper berth. It would make talk.

We was up in the morning in time to see our friends from New Hampshire get off at Tarpon Springs, which we reached at 6.53 A.M.

Several of our fellow passengers got off at Clearwater and some at Belleair, where the train backs right up to the door of the mammoth hotel. Belleair is the winter headquarters for the golf dudes and everybody that got off there had their bag of sticks, as many as ten and twelve in a bag. Women and all. When I was a young man we called it shinny and only needed one club to play with and about one game of it would of been a-plenty for some of these dudes, the way we played it.

The train pulled into St. Petersburg at 8.20 and when we got off the train you would think they was a riot, what with all the darkies barking for the different hotels.

I said to Mother, I said:

"It is a good thing we have got a place picked out to go to and don't have to choose a hotel, as it would be hard to choose amongst them if every one of them is the best."

She laughed.

We found a jitney and I give him the address of the room my son-in-law had got for us and soon we was there and introduced ourselves to the lady that owns the house, a young widow about forty-eight years of age. She showed us our room, which was light and airy with a comfortable bed and bureau and washstand. It was twelve dollars a week, but the location was good, only three blocks from Williams Park.

St. Pete is what folks call the town, though they also call it the Sunshine City, as they claim they's no other place in the country where they's fewer days when Old Sol don't smile down on Mother Earth, and one of the newspapers gives away all their copies free every day when the sun don't shine. They claim to of only give them away some sixty-odd times in the last eleven years. Another nickname they have got for the town is "the Poor Man's Palm Beach," but I guess they's men that comes there that could borrow as much from the bank as some of the Willie boys over to the other Palm Beach.

During our stay we paid a visit to the Lewis Tent City, which is the headquarters for the Tin Can Tourists. But maybe you ain't heard about them. Well, they are an organization that takes their vacation trips by auto and carries everything with them. That is, they bring along their tents to sleep in and cook in and they don't patronize no hotels or cafeterias, but they have got to be bona fide auto campers or they can't belong to the organization.

They tell me they's over 200,000 members to it and they call themselves the Tin Canners on account of most of their food being put up in tin cans. One couple we seen in the Tent City was a couple from Brady, Texas, named Mr. and Mrs. Pence, which the old man is over eighty years of age and they had come in their auto all the way from home, a distance of 1,641 miles. They took five weeks for the trip, Mr. Pence driving the entire distance.

The Tin Canners hails from every State in the Union and in the summer time they visit places like New England and the Great Lakes region, but in the winter the most of them comes to Florida and scatters all over the State. While we was down there, they was a national convention of them at Gainesville, Florida, and they elected a Fredonia, New York, man as their

president. His title is Royal Tin Can Opener of the World. They
have got a song wrote up which everybody has got to learn it
before they are a member:

> "*The tin can forever! Hurrah, boys! Hurrah!*
> *Up with the tin can! Down with the foe!*
> *We will rally round the campfire, we'll rally once again,*
> *Shouting, 'We auto camp forever!'*"

That is something like it. And the members has also got to
have a tin can fastened on to the front of their machine.

I asked Mother how she would like to travel around that way
and she said:

"Fine, but not with an old rattle brain like you driving."

"Well," I said, "I am eight years younger than this Mr. Pence
who drove here from Texas."

"Yes," she said, "but he is old enough to not be skittish."

You can't get ahead of Mother.

Well, one of the first things we done in St. Petersburg was to
go to the Chamber of Commerce and register our names and
where we was from as they's a great rivalry amongst the different States in regards to the number of their citizens visiting in
town and of course our little State don't stand much of a show,
but still every little bit helps, as the fella says. All and all, the man
told us, they was eleven thousand names registered, Ohio lead-
ing with some fifteen hundred-odd and New York State next
with twelve hundred. Then come Michigan, Pennsylvania and
so on down, with one man each from Cuba and Nevada.

The first night we was there, they was a meeting of the New
York-New Jersey Society at the Congregational Church and a
man from Ogdensburg, New York State, made the talk. His
subject was Rainbow Chasing. He is a Rotarian and a very con-
victing speaker, though I forget his name.

Our first business, of course, was to find a place to eat and after
trying several places we run on to a cafeteria on Central Avenue

that suited us up and down. We eat pretty near all our meals there and it averaged about two dollars per day for the two of us, but the food was well cooked and everything nice and clean. A man don't mind paying the price if things is clean and well cooked.

On the third day of February, which is Mother's birthday, we spread ourselves and eat supper at the Poinsettia Hotel and they charged us seventy-five cents for a sirloin steak that wasn't hardly big enough for one.

I said to Mother: "Well," I said, "I guess it's a good thing every day ain't your birthday or we would be in the poorhouse."

"No," says Mother, "because if every day was my birthday, I would be old enough by this time to of been in my grave long ago."

You can't get ahead of Mother.

In the hotel they had a card-room where they was several men and ladies playing five hundred and this new fangled whist bridge. We also seen a place where they was dancing, so I asked Mother would she like to trip the light fantastic toe and she said no, she was too old to squirm like you have got to do now days. We watched some of the young folks at it awhile till Mother got disgusted and said we would have to see a good movie to take the taste out of our mouth. Mother is a great movie heroyne and we go twice a week here at home.

But I want to tell you about the Park. The second day we was there we visited the Park, which is a good deal like the one in Tampa, only bigger, and they's more fun goes on here every day than you could shake a stick at. In the middle they's a big bandstand and chairs for the folks to set and listen to the concerts, which they give you music for all tastes, from Dixie up to classical pieces like Hearts and Flowers.

Then all around they's places marked off for different sports and games—chess and checkers and dominoes for folks that enjoys those kind of games, and roque and horse-shoes for the nimbler ones. I used to pitch a pretty fair shoe myself, but ain't done much of it in the last twenty years.

Well, anyway, we both bought a membership ticket in the club which costs one dollar for the season, and they tell me that up to a couple years ago it was fifty cents, but they had to raise it to keep out the riffraff.

Well, Mother and I put in a great day watching the pitchers and she wanted I should get in the game, but I told her I was all out of practice and would make a fool of myself, though I seen several men pitching who I guess I could take their measure without no practice. However, they was some good pitchers, too, and one boy from Akron, Ohio, who could certainly throw a pretty shoe. They told me it looked like he would win the championship of the United States in the February tournament. We come away a few days before they held that and I never did hear if he win. I forget his name, but he was a clean cut young fella and he has got a brother in Cleveland that's a Rotarian.

Well, we just stood around and watched the different games for two or three days and finally I set down in a checker game with a man named Weaver from Danville, Illinois. He was a pretty fair checker player, but he wasn't no match for me, and I hope that don't sound like bragging. But I always could hold my own on a checker-board and the folks around here will tell you the same thing. I played with this Weaver pretty near all morning for two or three mornings and he beat me one game and the only other time it looked like he had a chance, the noon whistle blowed and we had to quit and go to dinner.

While I was playing checkers, Mother would set and listen to the band, as she loves music, classical or no matter what kind, but anyway she was setting there one day and between selections the woman next to her opened up a conversation. She was a woman about Mother's own age, seventy or seventy-one, and finally she asked Mother's name and Mother told her her name and where she was from and Mother asked her the same question, and who do you think the woman was?

Well, sir, it was the wife of Frank M. Hartsell, the man who was engaged to Mother till I stepped in and cut him out, fifty-two years ago!

Yes, sir!

You can imagine Mother's surprise! And Mrs. Hartsell was surprised, too, when Mother told her she had once been friends with her husband, though Mother didn't say how close friends they had been, or that Mother and I was the cause of Hartsell going out West. But that's what we was. Hartsell left his town a month after the engagement was broke off and ain't never been back since. He had went out to Michigan and become a veterinary, and that is where he had settled down, in Hillsdale, Michigan, and finally married his wife.

Well, Mother screwed up her courage to ask if Frank was still living and Mrs. Hartsell took her over to where they was pitching horse-shoes and there was old Frank, waiting his turn. And he knowed Mother as soon as he seen her, though it was over fifty years. He said he knowed her by her eyes.

"Why, it's Lucy Frost!" he says, and he throwed down his shoes and quit the game.

Then they come over and hunted me up and I will confess I wouldn't of knowed him. Him and I is the same age to the month, but he seems to show it more, some way. He is balder for one thing. And his beard is all white, where mine has still got a streak of brown in it. The very first thing I said to him, I said:

"Well, Frank, that beard of yours makes me feel like I was back north. It looks like a regular blizzard."

"Well," he said, "I guess yourn would be just as white if you had it dry cleaned."

But Mother wouldn't stand that.

"Is that so!" she said to Frank. "Well, Charley ain't had no tobacco in his mouth for over ten years!"

And I ain't!

Well, I excused myself from the checker game and it was pretty close to noon, so we decided to all have dinner together and they was nothing for it only we must try their cafeteria on Third Avenue. It was a little more expensive than ours and not near as good, I thought. I and Mother had about the same dinner we had been having every day and our bill was $1.10. Frank's check was $1.20 for he and his wife. The same meal wouldn't of cost them more than a dollar at our place.

After dinner we made them come up to our house and we all set in the parlor, which the young woman had give us the use of to entertain company. We begun talking over old times and Mother said she was a-scared Mrs. Hartsell would find it tiresome listening to we three talk over old times, but as it turned out they wasn't much chance for nobody else to talk with Mrs. Hartsell in the company. I have heard lots of women that could go it, but Hartsell's wife takes the cake of all the women I ever seen. She told us the family history of everybody in the State of Michigan and bragged for a half hour about her son, who she said is in the drug business in Grand Rapids, and a Rotarian.

When I and Hartsell could get a word in edgeways we joked one another back and forth and I chafed him about being a horse doctor.

"Well, Frank," I said, "you look pretty prosperous, so I suppose they's been plenty of glanders around Hillsdale."

"Well," he said, "I've managed to make more than a fair living. But I've worked pretty hard."

"Yes," I said, "and I suppose you get called out all hours of the night to attend births and so on."

Mother made me shut up.

Well, I thought they wouldn't never go home and I and Mother was in misery trying to keep awake, as the both of us generally always takes a nap after dinner. Finally they went, after we had made an engagement to meet them in the Park the next morning, and Mrs. Hartsell also invited us to come to their place the next night and play five hundred. But she had forgot that they was a meeting of the Michigan Society that evening, so it was not till two evenings later that we had our first card game.

Hartsell and his wife lived in a house on Third Avenue North and had a private setting room besides their bedroom. Mrs. Hartsell couldn't quit talking about their private setting room like it was something wonderful. We played cards with them, with Mother and Hartsell partners aginst his wife and I. Mrs. Hartsell is a miserable card player and we certainly got the worst of it.

After the game she brought out a dish of oranges and we had to pretend it was just what we wanted, though oranges down there is like a young man's whiskers; you enjoy them at first, but they get to be a pesky nuisance.

We played cards again the next night at our place with the same partners and I and Mrs. Hartsell was beat again. Mother and Hartsell was full of compliments for each other on what a good team they made, but they both of them knowed well enough where the secret of their success laid. I guess all and all we must of played ten different evenings and they was only one night when Mrs. Hartsell and I come out ahead. And that one night wasn't no fault of hern.

When we had been down there about two weeks, we spent one evening as their guest in the Congregational Church, at a social give by the Michigan Society. A talk was made by a man named Bitting of Detroit, Michigan, on How I was Cured of Story Telling. He is a big man in the Rotarians and give a witty talk.

A woman named Mrs. Oxford rendered some selections

which Mrs. Hartsell said was grand opera music, but whatever they was my daughter Edie could of give her cards and spades and not made such a hullaballoo about it neither.

Then they was a ventriloquist from Grand Rapids and a young woman about forty-five years of age that mimicked different kinds of birds. I whispered to Mother that they all sounded like a chicken, but she nudged me to shut up.

After the show we stopped in a drug store and I set up the refreshments and it was pretty close to ten o'clock before we finally turned in. Mother and I would of preferred tending the movies, but Mother said we musn't offend Mrs. Hartsell, though I asked her had we came to Florida to enjoy ourselves or to just not offend an old chatter-box from Michigan.

I felt sorry for Hartsell one morning. The women folks both had an engagement down to the chiropodist's and I run across Hartsell in the Park and he foolishly offered to play me checkers.

It was him that suggested it, not me, and I guess he repented himself before we had played one game. But he was too stubborn to give up and set there while I beat him game after game and the worst part of it was that a crowd of folks had got in the habit of watching me play and there they all was, looking on, and finally they seen what a fool Frank was making of himself, and they began to chafe him and pass remarks. Like one of them said:

"Who ever told you you was a checker player!"

And:

"You might maybe be good for tiddle-de-winks, but not checkers!"

I almost felt like letting him beat me a couple games. But the crowd would of knowed it was a put up job.

Well, the women folks joined us in the Park and I wasn't going to mention our little game, but Hartsell told about it himself and admitted he wasn't no match for me.

"Well," said Mrs. Hartsell, "checkers ain't much of a game

anyway, is it?" She said: "It's more of a children's game, ain't it? At least, I know my boy's children used to play it a good deal."

"Yes, ma'am," I said. "It's a children's game the way your husband plays it, too."

Mother wanted to smooth things over, so she said:

"Maybe they's other games where Frank can beat you."

"Yes," said Mrs. Hartsell, "and I bet he could beat you pitching horse-shoes."

"Well," I said, "I would give him a chance to try, only I ain't pitched a shoe in over sixteen years."

"Well," said Hartsell, "I ain't played checkers in twenty years."

"You ain't never played it," I said.

"Anyway," says Frank, "Lucy and I is your master at five hundred."

Well, I could of told him why that was, but had decency enough to hold my tongue.

It had got so now that he wanted to play cards every night and when I or Mother wanted to go to a movie, any one of us would have to pretend we had a headache and then trust to goodness that they wouldn't see us sneak into the theater. I don't mind playing cards when my partner keeps their mind on the game, but you take a woman like Hartsell's wife and how can they play cards when they have got to stop every couple seconds and brag about their son in Grand Rapids?

Well, the New York-New Jersey Society announced that they was goin to give a social evening too and I said to Mother, I said:

"Well, that is one evening when we will have an excuse not to play five hundred."

"Yes," she said, "but we will have to ask Frank and his wife to go to the social with us as they asked us to go to the Michigan social."

"Well," I said, "I had rather stay home than drag that chatterbox everywheres we go."

So Mother said:

"You are getting too cranky. Maybe she does talk a little too much but she is good hearted. And Frank is always good company."

So I said:

"I suppose if he is such good company you wished you had of married him."

Mother laughed and said I sounded like I was jealous. Jealous of a cow doctor!

Anyway we had to drag them along to the social and I will say that we give them a much better entertainment than they had given us.

Judge Lane of Paterson made a fine talk on business conditions and a Mrs. Newell of Westfield imitated birds, only you could really tell what they was the way she done it. Two young women from Red Bank sung a choral selection and we clapped them back and they gave us Home to Our Mountains and Mother and Mrs. Hartsell both had tears in their eyes. And Hartsell, too.

Well, some way or another the chairman got wind that I was there and asked me to make a talk and I wasn't even going to get up, but Mother made me, so I got up and said:

"Ladies and gentlemen," I said. "I didn't expect to be called on for a speech on an occasion like this or no other occasion as I do not set myself up as a speech maker, so will have to do the best I can, which I often say is the best anybody can do."

Then I told them the story about Pat and the motorcycle, using the brogue, and it seemed to tickle them and I told them one or two other stories, but altogether I wasn't on my feet more than twenty or twenty-five minutes and you ought to of heard the clapping and hollering when I set down. Even Mrs. Hartsell admitted that I am quite a speechifier and said if I ever went to Grand Rapids, Michigan, her son would make me talk to the Rotarians.

When it was over, Hartsell wanted we should go to their house and play cards, but his wife reminded him that it was after 9.30 P.M., rather a late hour to start a card game, but he had went crazy on the subject of cards, probably because he didn't have to play partners with his wife. Anyway, we got rid of them and went home to bed.

It was the next morning, when we met over to the Park, that Mrs. Hartsell made the remark that she wasn't getting no exercise so I suggested that why didn't she take part in the roque game.

She said she had not played a game of roque in twenty years, but if Mother would play she would play. Well, at first Mother wouldn't hear of it, but finally consented, more to please Mrs. Hartsell than anything else.

Well, they had a game with a Mrs. Ryan from Eagle, Nebraska, and a young Mrs. Morse from Rutland, Vermont, who Mother had met down to the chiropodist's. Well, Mother couldn't hit a flea and they all laughed at her and I couldn't help from laughing at her myself and finally she quit and said her back was too lame to stoop over. So they got another lady and kept on playing and soon Mrs. Hartsell was the one everybody was laughing at, as she had a long shot to hit the black ball, and as she made the effort her teeth fell out on to the court. I never seen a woman so flustered in my life. And I never heard so much laughing, only Mrs. Hartsell didn't join in and she was madder than a hornet and wouldn't play no more, so the game broke up.

Mrs. Hartwell went home without speaking to nobody, but Hartsell stayed around and finally he said to me, he said:

"Well, I played you checkers the other day and you beat me bad and now what do you say if you and me play a game of horseshoes?"

I told him I hadn't pitched a shoe in sixteen years, but Mother said:

"Go ahead and play. You used to be good at it and maybe it will come back to you."

Well, to make a long story short, I give in. I oughtn't to of never tried it, as I hadn't pitched a shoe in sixteen years, and I only done it to humor Hartsell.

Before we started, Mother patted me on the back and told me to do my best, so we started in and I seen right off that I was in for it, as I hadn't pitched a shoe in sixteen years and didn't have my distance. And besides, the plating had wore off the shoes so that they was points right where they stuck into my thumb and I hadn't throwed more than two or three times when my thumb was raw and it pretty near killed me to hang on to the shoe, let alone pitch it.

Well, Hartsell throws the awkwardest shoe I ever seen pitched and to see him pitch you wouldn't think he would ever come nowheres near, but he is also the luckiest pitcher I ever seen and he made some pitches where the shoe lit five and six feet short and then schoonered up and was a ringer. They's no use trying to beat that kind of luck.

They was a pretty fair size crowd watching us and four or five other ladies besides Mother, and it seems like, when Hartsell pitches, he has got to chew and it kept the ladies on the anxious seat as he don't seem to care which way he is facing when he leaves go.

You would think a man as old as him would of learnt more manners.

Well, to make a long story short, I was just beginning to get my distance when I had to give up on account of my thumb, which I showed it to Hartsell and he seen I couldn't go on, as it was raw and bleeding. Even if I could of stood it to go on myself, Mother wouldn't of allowed it after she seen my thumb. So anyway I quit and Hartsell said the score was nineteen to six, but I don't know what it was. Or don't care, neither.

Well, Mother and I went home and I said I hoped we

was through with the Hartsells and I was sick and tired of them, but it seemed like she had promised we would go over to their house that evening for another game of their everlasting cards.

Well, my thumb was giving me considerable pain and I felt kind of out of sorts and I guess maybe I forgot myself, but anyway, when we was about through playing Hartsell made the remark that he wouldn't never lose a game of cards if he could always have Mother for a partner.

So I said:

"Well, you had a chance fifty years ago to always have her for a partner, but you wasn't man enough to keep her."

I was sorry the minute I had said it and Hartsell didn't know what to say and for once his wife couldn't say nothing. Mother tried to smooth things over by making the remark that I must of had something stronger than tea or I wouldn't talk so silly. But Mrs. Hartsell had froze up like an iceberg and hardly said good night to us and I bet her and Frank put in a pleasant hour after we was gone.

As we was leaving, Mother said to him: "Never mind Charley's nonsense, Frank. He is just mad because you beat him all hollow pitching horseshoes and playing cards."

She said that to make up for my slip, but at the same time she certainly riled me. I tried to keep ahold of myself, but as soon as we was out of the house she had to open up the subject and begun to scold me for the break I had made.

Well, I wasn't in no mood to be scolded. So I said:

"I guess he is such a wonderful pitcher and card player that you wished you had married him."

"Well," she said, "at least he ain't a baby to give up pitching because his thumb has got a few scratches."

"And how about you," I said, "making a fool of yourself on that roque court and then pretending your back is lame and you can't play no more!"

"Yes," she said, "but when you hurt your thumb I didn't laugh at you, and why did you laugh at me when I sprained my back?"

"Who could help from laughing!" I said.

"Well," she said, "Frank Hartsell didn't laugh."

"Well," I said, "why didn't you marry him?"

"Well," said Mother, "I almost wished I had!"

"And I wished so, too!" I said.

"I'll remember that!" said Mother, and that's the last word she said to me for two days.

We seen the Hartsells the next day in the Park and I was willing to apologize, but they just nodded to us. And a couple days later we heard they had left for Orlando, where they have got relatives.

I wished they had went there in the first place.

Mother and I made it up setting on a bench.

"Listen, Charley," she said. "This is our Golden Honeymoon and we don't want the whole thing spoilt with a silly old quarrel."

"Well," I said, "did you mean that about wishing you had married Hartsell?"

"Of course not," she said, "that is, if you didn't mean that you wished I had, too."

So I said:

"I was just tired and all wrought up. I thank God you chose me instead of him as they's no other woman in the world who I could of lived with all these years."

"How about Mrs. Hartsell?" says Mother.

"Good gracious!" I said. "Imagine being married to a woman that plays five hundred like she does and drops her teeth on the roque court!"

"Well," said Mother, "it wouldn't be no worse than being married to a man that expectorates towards ladies and is such a fool in a checker game."

So I put my arm around her shoulder and she stroked my hand and I guess we got kind of spoony.

They was two days left of our stay in St. Petersburg and the next to the last day Mother introduced me to a Mrs. Kendall from Kingston, Rhode Island, who she had met at the chiropodist's.

Mrs. Kendall made us acquainted with her husband, who is in the grocery business. They have got two sons and five grandchildren and one great-grandchild. One of their sons lives in Providence and is way up in the Elks as well as a Rotarian.

We found them very congenial people and we played cards with them the last two nights we was there. They was both experts and I only wished we had met them sooner instead of running into the Hartsells. But the Kendalls will be there again next winter and we will see more of them, that is, if we decide to make the trip again.

We left the Sunshine City on the eleventh day of February, at 11 A.M. This give us a day trip through Florida and we seen all the country we had passed through at night on the way down.

We reached Jacksonville at 7 P.M. and pulled out of there at 8:10 P.M. We reached Fayetteville, North Carolina, at nine o'clock the following morning, and reached Washington, D.C., at 6:30 P.M., laying over there half an hour.

We reached Trenton at 11.01 P.M. and had wired ahead to my daughter and son-in-law and they met us at the train and we went to their house and they put us up for the night. John would of made us stay up all night, telling about our trip, but Edie said we must be tired and made us go to bed. That's my daughter.

The next day we took our train for home and arrived safe and sound, having been gone just one month and a day.

Here comes Mother, so I guess I better shut up.

HORSESHOES

The series ended Tuesday, but I had stayed in Philadelphia an extra day on the chance of there being some follow-up stuff worth sending. Nothing had broken loose; so I filed some stuff about what the Athletics and the Giants were going to do with their dough, and then caught the eight o'clock train for Chicago.

Having passed up supper in order to get my story away and grab the train, I went to the buffet car right after I'd planted my grips. I sat down at one of the tables and ordered a sandwich. Four salesmen were playing rum at the other table and all the chairs in the car were occupied; so it didn't surprise me when somebody flopped down in the seat opposite me.

I looked up from my paper and with a little thrill recognized my companion. Now I've been experting round the country with ball players so much that it doesn't usually excite me to meet one face to face, even if he's a star. I can talk with Tyrus without getting all fussed up. But this particular player had jumped from obscurity to fame so suddenly and had played such an important though brief part in the recent argument between the Macks and McGraws that I couldn't help being a little awed by his proximity.

It was none other than Grimes, the utility outfielder Connie had been forced to use in the last game because of the injury to Joyce—Grimes, whose miraculous catch in the eleventh inning had robbed Parker of a home run and the Giants of victory, and

whose own homer, a fluky one—had given the Athletics another
World's Championship.

I had met Grimes one day during the spring he was with the
Cubs, but I knew he wouldn't remember me. A ball player never
recalls a reporter's face on less than six introductions or his name
on less than twenty. However, I resolved to speak to him, and
had just mustered sufficient courage to open a conversation when
he saved me the trouble.

"Whose picture have they got there?" he asked, pointing to
my paper.

"Speed Parker's," I replied.

"What do they say about him?" asked Grimes.

"I'll read it to you," I said:

" 'Speed Parker, McGraw's great third baseman, is ill in a local
hospital with nervous prostration, the result of the strain of the
World Series, in which he played such a stellar rôle. Parker is in
such a dangerous condition that no one is allowed to see him.
Members of the New York team and fans from Gotham called
at the hospital to-day, but were unable to gain admittance to his
ward. Philadelphians hope he will recover speedily and will suffer
no permanent ill effects from his sickness, for he won their admiration by his work in the series, though he was on a rival team.
A lucky catch by Grimes, the Athletics' substitute outfielder,
was all that prevented Parker from winning the title for New
York. According to Manager Mack, of the champions, the series
would have been over in four games but for Parker's wonderful
exhibition of nerve and——' "

"That'll be aplenty," Grimes interrupted. "And that's just
what you might expect from one o' them doughheaded reporters. If all the baseball writers was where they belonged they'd
have to build an annex to Matteawan."

I kept my temper with very little effort—it takes more than a
peevish ball player's remarks to insult one of our fraternity; but
I didn't exactly understand his peeve.

"Doesn't Parker deserve the bouquet?" I asked.

"Oh, they can boost him all they want to," said Grimes; "but when they call that catch lucky and don't mention the fact that Parker is the luckiest guy in the world, somethin' must be wrong with 'em. Did you see the serious?"

"No," I lied glibly, hoping to draw from him the cause of his grouch.

"Well," he said, "you sure missed somethin'. They never was a serious like it before and they won't never be one again. It went the full seven games and every game was a bear. They was one big innin' every day and Parker was the big cheese in it. Just as Connie says, the Ath-a-letics would of cleaned 'em in four games but for Parker; but it wasn't because he's a great ball player—it was because he was born with a knife, fork and spoon in his mouth, and a rabbit's foot hung round his neck.

"You may not know it, but I'm Grimes, the guy that made the lucky catch. I'm the guy that won the serious with a hit— a homerun hit; and I'm here to tell you that if I'd had one-tenth o' Parker's luck they'd of heard about me long before yesterday. They say my homer was lucky. Maybe it was; but, believe me, it was time things broke for me. They been breakin' for him all his life."

"Well," I said, "his luck must have gone back on him if he's in a hospital with nervous prostration."

"Nervous prostration nothin'," said Grimes. "He's in a hospital because his face is all out o' shape and he's ashamed to appear on the street. I don't usually do so much talkin' and I'm ravin' a little to-night because I've had a couple o' drinks; but——"

"Have another," said I, ringing for the waiter, "and talk some more."

"I made two hits yesterday," Grimes went on, "but the crowd only seen one. I busted up the game and the serious with the one they seen. The one they didn't see was the one I busted up a guy's map with—and Speed Parker was the guy. That's why he's in a hospital. He may be able to play ball next year; but I'll bet my share o' the dough that McGraw won't reco'nize him when he shows up at Marlin in the spring."

"When did this come off?" I asked. "And why?"

"It come off outside the clubhouse after yesterday's battle," he said; "and I hit him because he called me a name—a name I won't stand for from him."

"What did he call you?" I queried, expecting to hear one of the delicate epithets usually applied by conquered to conqueror on the diamond.

" 'Horseshoes!' " was Grimes' amazing reply.

"But, good Lord!" I remonstrated, "I've heard of ball players calling each other that, and Lucky Stiff, and Fourleaf Clover, ever since I was a foot high, and I never knew them to start fights about it."

"Well," said Grimes, "I might as well give you all the dope; and then if you don't think I was justified I'll pay your fare from here to wherever you're goin'. I don't want you to think I'm kickin' about trifles—or that I'm kickin' at all, for that matter. I just want to prove to you that he didn't have no license to pull that Horseshoes stuff on me and that I only give him what was comin' to him."

"Go ahead and shoot," said I.

"Give us some more o' the same," said Grimes to the passing waiter. And then he told me about it.

Maybe you've heard that me and Speed Parker was raised in the same town—Ishpeming, Michigan. We was kids together, and though he done all the devilment I got all the lickin's. When we was about twelve years old Speed throwed a rotten egg at the teacher and I got expelled. That made me sick o' schools and I wouldn't never go to one again, though my ol' man beat me up and the truant officers threatened to have me hung.

Well, while Speed was learnin' what was the principal products

o' New Hampshire and Texas I was workin' round the freight-
house and drivin' a dray.

We'd both been playin' ball all our lives; and when the town
organized a semi-pro club we got jobs with it. We was to draw
two bucks apiece for each game and they played every Sunday.
We played four games before we got our first pay. They was a
hole in my pants pocket as big as the home plate, but I forgot
about it and put the dough in there. It wasn't there when I got
home. Speed didn't have no hole in his pocket—you can bet on
that! Afterward the club hired a good outfielder and I was
canned. They was huntin' for another third baseman too; but, o'
course, they didn't find none and Speed held his job.

The next year they started the Northern Peninsula League. We
landed with the home team. The league opened in May and
blowed up the third week in June. They paid off all the outsiders
first and then had just money enough left to settle with one of us
two Ishpeming guys. The night they done the payin' I was out
to my uncle's farm, so they settled with Speed and told me I'd
have to wait for mine. I'm still waitin'!

Gene Higgins, who was manager o' the Battle Creek Club,
lived in Houghton, and that winter we goes over and strikes him
for a job. He give it to us and we busted in together two years
ago last spring.

I had a good year down there. I hit over .300 and stole all the
bases in sight. Speed got along good too, and they was several
big-league scouts lookin' us over. The Chicago Cubs bought
Speed outright and four clubs put in a draft for me. Three of 'em
—Cleveland and the New York Giants and the Boston Nationals
—needed outfielders bad, and it would of been a pipe for me to of
made good with any of 'em. But who do you think got me? The
same Chicago Cubs; and the only outfielders they had at that
time was Schulte and Leach and Good and Williams, and Stewart,
and one or two others.

Well, I didn't figure I was any worse off than Speed. The Cubs had Zimmerman at third base and it didn't look like they was any danger of a busher beatin' him out; but Zimmerman goes and breaks his leg the second day o' the season—that's a year ago last April—and Speed jumps right in as a regular. Do you think anything like that could happen to Schulte or Leach, or any o' them outfielders? No sir! I wore out my uniform slidin' up and down the bench and wonderin' whether they'd ship me to Fort Worth or Siberia.

Now I want to tell you about the miserable luck Speed had right off the reel. He was playin' at St. Louis. They had a one-run lead in the eighth, when their pitcher walked Speed with one out. Saier hits a high fly to centre and Parker starts with the crack o' the bat. Both coachers was yellin' at him to go back, but he thought they was two out and he was clear round to third base when the ball came down. And Oakes muffs it! O' course he scored and the game was tied up.

Parker come in to the bench like he'd did something wonderful.

"Did you think they was two out?" ast Hank.

"No," says Speed, blushin'.

"Then what did you run for?" says Hank.

"I had a hunch he was goin' to drop the ball," says Speed; and Hank pretty near falls off the bench.

The next day he come up with one out and the sacks full, and the score tied in the sixth. He smashes one on the ground straight at Hauser and it looked like a cinch double play; but just as Hauser was goin' to grab it the ball hit a rough spot and hopped a mile over his head. It got between Oakes and Magee and went clear to the fence. Three guys scored and Speed pulled up at third. The papers come out and said the game was won by a three-bagger from the bat o' Parker, the Cubs' sensational kid third baseman. Gosh!

We go home to Chi and are havin' a hot battle with Pittsburgh. This time Speed's turn come when they was two on and two out, and Pittsburgh a run to the good—I think it was the eighth innin'. Cooper gives him a fast one and he hits it straight up in the air. O' course the runners started goin', but it looked hopeless because they wasn't no wind or high sky to bother anybody. Mowrey and Gibson both goes after the ball; and just as Mowrey was set for the catch Gibson bumps into him and they both fall down. Two runs scored and Speed got to second. Then what does he do but try to steal third—with two out too! And Gibson's peg pretty near hits the left field seats on the fly.

When Speed comes to the bench Hank says:

"If I was you I'd quit playin' ball and go to Monte Carlo."

"What for?" says Speed.

"You're so dam' lucky!" says Hank.

"So is Ty Cobb," says Speed. That's how he hated himself!

First trip to Cincy we run into a couple of old Ishpeming boys. They took us out one night, and about twelve o'clock I said we'd have to go back to the hotel or we'd get fined. Speed said I had cold feet and he stuck with the boys. I went back alone and Hank caught me comin' in and put a fifty-dollar plaster on me. Speed stayed out all night long and Hank never knowed it. I says to myself: "Wait till he gets out there and tries to play ball without no sleep!" But the game that day was called off on account o' rain. Can you beat it?

I remember what he got away with the next afternoon the same as though it happened yesterday. In the second innin' they walked him with nobody down, and he took a big lead off first base like he always does. Benton throwed over there three or four times to scare him back, and the last time he throwed, Hobby hid the ball. The coacher seen it and told Speed to hold the bag; but he didn't pay no attention. He started leadin' right off again and Hobby tried to tag him, but the ball slipped out of his hand and rolled about a yard away. Parker had plenty o' time to get back; but, instead o' that, he starts for second. Hobby picked up the ball and shot it down to Groh—and Groh made a square muff.

Parker slides into the bag safe and then gets up and throws out his chest like he'd made the greatest play ever. When the ball's throwed back to Benton, Speed leads off about thirty foot and stands there in a trance. Clarke signs for a pitch-out and pegs down to second to nip him. He was caught flatfooted—that is, he would of been with a decent throw; but Clarke's peg went pretty near to Latonia. Speed scored and strutted over to receive our hearty congratulations. Some o' the boys was laughin' and he thought they was laughin' with him instead of at him.

It was in the ninth, though, that he got by with one o' the worst I ever seen. The Reds was a run behind and Marsans was on third base with two out. Hobby, I think it was, hit one on the ground right at Speed and he picked it up clean. The crowd all got up and started for the exits. Marsans run toward the plate in the faint hope that the peg to first would be wild. All of a sudden the boys on the Cincy bench began yellin' at him to slide, and he done so. He was way past the plate when Speed's throw got to Archer. The bonehead had shot the ball home instead o' to first base, thinkin' they was only one down. We was all crazy, believin' his nut play had let 'em tie it up; but he comes tearin' in, tellin' Archer to tag Marsans. So Jim walks over and tags the Cuban, who was brushin' off his uniform.

"You're out!" says Klem. "You never touched the plate."

I guess Marsans knowed the umps was right because he didn't make much of a holler. But Speed sure got a pannin' in the club-house.

"I suppose you knowed he was goin' to miss the plate!" says Hank sarcastic as he could.

Everybody on the club roasted him, but it didn't do no good.

Well, you know what happened to me. I only got into one game with the Cubs—one afternoon when Leach was sick. We was playin' the Boston bunch and Tyler was workin' against us. I always had trouble with lefthanders and this was one of his good days. I couldn't see what he throwed up there. I got one foul durin' the afternoon's entertainment; and the wind was blowin' a hundred-mile gale, so that the best outfielder in the world couldn't judge a fly ball. That Boston bunch must of hit fifty of 'em and they all come to my field.

If I caught any I've forgot about it. Couple o' days after that I got notice o' my release to Indianapolis.

Parker kept right on all season doin' the blamedest things you ever heard of and gettin' by with 'em. One o' the boys told me about it later. If they was playin' a double-header in St. Louis, with the thermometer at 130 degrees, he'd get put out by the umps in the first innin' o' the first game. If he started to steal the catcher'd drop the pitch or somebody'd muff the throw. If he hit a pop fly the sun'd get in somebody's eyes. If he took a swell third strike with the bases full the umps would call it a ball. If he cut first base by twenty feet the umps would be readin' the mornin' paper.

Zimmerman's leg mended, so that he was all right by June; and then Saier got sick and they tried Speed at first base. He'd never saw the bag before; but things kept on breakin' for him and he played it like a house afire. The Cubs copped the pennant and Speed got in on the big dough, besides playin' a whale of a game through the whole serious.

Speed and me both went back to Ishpeming to spend the winter—though the Lord knows it ain't no winter resort. Our homes was there; and besides, in my case, they was a certain girl livin' in the old burg.

Parker, o' course, was the hero and the swell guy when we got home. He'd been in the World Serious and had plenty o' dough in his kick. I come home with nothin' but my suitcase and a hard-luck story, which I kept to myself. I hadn't even went good enough in Indianapolis to be sure of a job there again.

That fall—last fall—an uncle o' Speed's died over in the Soo and left him ten thousand bucks. I had an uncle down in the Lower Peninsula who was worth five times that much—but he had good health!

This girl I spoke about was the prettiest thing I ever see. I'd went with her in the old days, and when I blew back I found she was still strong for me. They wasn't a great deal o' variety in Ishpeming for a girl to pick from. Her and I went to the dance every Saturday night and to church Sunday nights. I called on her Wednesday evenin's, besides takin' her to all the shows that come along—rotten as the most o' them was.

I never knowed Speed was makin' a play for this doll till along last Feb'uary. The minute I see what was up I got busy. I took her out sleigh-ridin' and kept her out in the cold till she'd promised to marry me. We set the date for this fall—I figured I'd know better where I was at by that time.

Well, we didn't make no secret o' bein' engaged; down in the poolroom one night Speed come up and congratulated me. He says:

"You got a swell girl, Dick! I wouldn't mind bein' in your place. You're mighty lucky to cop her out—you old Horseshoes, you!"

"Horseshoes!" I says. "You got a fine license to call anybody Horseshoes! I suppose you ain't never had no luck?"

"Not like you," he says.

I was feelin' too good about grabbin' the girl to get sore at the time; but when I got to thinkin' about it a few minutes afterward it made me mad clear through. What right did that bird have to talk about me bein' lucky?

Speed was playin' freeze-out at a table near the door, and when I started home some o' the boys with him says:

"Good night, Dick."

I said good night and then Speed looked up.

"Good night, Horseshoes!" he says.

That got my nanny this time.

"Shut up, you lucky stiff!" I says. "If you wasn't so dam' lucky you'd be sweepin' the streets." Then I walks on out.

I was too busy with the girl to see much o' Speed after that. He left home about the middle o' the month to go to Tampa with the Cubs. I got notice from Indianapolis that I was sold to Baltimore. I didn't care much about goin' there and I wasn't anxious to leave home under the circumstances, so I didn't report till late.

When I read in the papers along in April that Speed had been traded to Boston for a couple o' pitchers I thought: "Gee! He must of lost his rabbit's foot!" Because, even if the Cubs didn't cop again, they'd have a city serious with the White Sox and get a bunch o' dough that way. And they wasn't no chance in the world for the Boston Club to get nothin' but their salaries.

It wasn't another month, though, till Shafer, o' the Giants, quit baseball and McGraw was up against it for a third baseman. Next thing I knowed Speed was traded to New York and was with another winner—for they never was out o' first place all season.

I was gettin' along all right at Baltimore and Dunnie liked me; so I felt like I had somethin' more than just a one-year job—somethin' I could get married on. It was all framed that the weddin' was comin' off as soon as this season was over; so you can believe I was pullin' for October to hurry up and come.

One day in August, two months ago, Dunnie come in the clubhouse and handed me the news.

"Rube Oldring's busted his leg," he says, "and he's out for the rest o' the season. Connie's got a youngster named Joyce that he can stick in there, but he's got to have an extra outfielder. He's made me a good proposition for you and I'm goin' to let you go. It'll be pretty soft for you, because they got the pennant cinched and they'll cut you in on the big money."

"Yes," I says; "and when they're through with me they'll ship me to Hellangone, and I'll be draggin' down about seventy-five bucks a month next year."

"Nothin' like that," says Dunnie. "If he don't want you next season he's got to ask for waivers; and if you get out o' the big league you come right back here. That's all framed."

So that's how I come to get with the Ath-a-letics. Connie give me a nice, comf'table seat in one corner o' the bench and I had the pleasure o' watchin' a real ball club perform once every afternoon and sometimes twice.

Connie told me that as soon as they had the flag cinched he was goin' to lay off some of his regulars and I'd get a chance to play.

Well, they cinched it the fourth day o' September and our next engagement was with Washin'ton on Labor Day. We had two games and I was in both of 'em. And I broke in with my usual lovely luck, because the pitchers I was ast to face was Boehling, a nasty lefthander, and this guy Johnson.

The mornin' game was Boehling's and he wasn't no worse than some o' the rest of his kind. I only whiffed once and would of had a triple if Milan hadn't run from here to New Orleans and stole one off me.

"I'm not boastin' about my first experience with Johnson though. They can't never tell me he throws them balls with his arm. He's got a gun concealed about his person and he shoots 'em up there. I was leadin' off in Murphy's place and the game was a little delayed in startin', because I'd watched the big guy warm up and wasn't in no hurry to get to that plate. Before I left the bench Connie says:

"Don't try to take no healthy swing. Just meet 'em and you'll get along better."

So I tried to just meet the first one he throwed; but when I stuck out my bat Henry was throwin' the pill back to Johnson. Then I thought: Maybe if I start swingin' now at the second one I'll hit the third one. So I let the second one come over and the umps guessed it was another strike, though I'll bet a thousand bucks he couldn't see it no more'n I could.

While Johnson was still windin' up to pitch again I started to swing—and the big cuss crosses me with a slow one. I lunged at it twice and missed it both times, and the force o' my wallop throwed me clean back to the bench. The Ath-a-letics was all laughin' at me and I laughed too, because I was glad that much of it was over.

McInnes gets a base hit off him in the second innin' and I ast him how he done it.

"He's a friend o' mine," says Jack, "and he lets up when he pitches to me."

I made up my mind right there that if I was goin' to be in the league next year I'd go out and visit Johnson this winter and get acquainted.

I wished before the day was over that I was hittin' in the catcher's place, because the fellers down near the tail-end of the battin' order only had to face him three times. He fanned me on three pitched balls again in the third, and when I come up in the sixth he scared me to death by pretty near beanin' me with the first one.

"Be careful!" says Henry. "He's gettin' pretty wild and he's liable to knock you away from your uniform."

"Don't he never curve one?" I ast.

"Sure!" says Henry. "Do you want to see his curve?"

"Yes," I says, knowin' the hook couldn't be no worse'n the fast one.

So he give me three hooks in succession and I missed 'em all; but I felt more comf'table than when I was duckin' his fast ball. In the ninth he hit my bat with a curve and the ball went on the ground to McBride. He booted it, but throwed me out easy—because I was so surprised at not havin' whiffed that I forgot to run!

Well, I went along like that for the rest o' the season, runnin'
up against the best pitchers in the league and not exactly mur-
derin' 'em. Everything I tried went wrong, and I was smart
enough to know that if anything had depended on the games I
wouldn't of been in there for two minutes. Joyce and Strunk and
Murphy wasn't jealous o' me a bit; but they was glad to take
turns restin', and I didn't care much how I went so long as I was
sure of a job next year.

I'd wrote to the girl a couple o' times askin' her to set the exact
date for our weddin'; but she hadn't paid no attention. She said
she was glad I was with the Ath-a-letics, but she thought the
Giants was goin' to beat us. I might of suspected from that that
somethin' was wrong, because not even a girl would pick the
Giants to trim that bunch of ourn. Finally, the day before the
serious started, I sent her a kind o' sassy letter sayin' I guessed it
was up to me to name the day, and askin' whether October twen-
tieth was all right. I told her to wire me yes or no.

I'd been readin' the dope about Speed all season, and I knowed
he'd had a whale of a year and that his luck was right with him;
but I never dreamed a man could have the Lord on his side as
strong as Speed did in that World's Serious! I might as well tell
you all the dope, so long as you wasn't there.

The first game was on our grounds and Connie give us a talkin'
to in the clubhouse beforehand.

"The shorter this serious is," he says, "the better for us. If it's
a long serious we're goin' to have trouble, because McGraw's
got five pitchers he can work and we've got about three; so I
want you boys to go at 'em from the jump and play 'em off their
feet. Don't take things easy, because it ain't goin' to be no snap.
Just because we've licked 'em before ain't no sign we'll do it this
time."

Then he calls me to one side and ast me what I knowed about
Parker.

"You was with the Cubs when he was, wasn't you?" he says.

"Yes," I says; "and he's the luckiest stiff you ever seen! If he got stewed and fell in the gutter he'd catch a fish."

"I don't like to hear a good ball player called lucky," says Connie. "He must have a lot of ability or McGraw wouldn't use him regular. And he's been hittin' about .340 and played a bang-up game at third base. That can't be all luck."

"Wait till you see him," I says; "and if you don't say he's the luckiest guy in the world you can sell me to the Boston Bloomer Girls. He's so lucky," I says, "that if they traded him to the St. Louis Browns they'd have the pennant cinched by the Fourth o' July."

And I'll bet Connie was willin' to agree with me before it was over.

Well, the Chief worked against the Big Rube in that game. We beat 'em, but they give us a battle and it was Parker that made it close. We'd gone along nothin' and nothin' till the seventh, and then Rube walks Collins and Baker lifts one over that little old wall. You'd think by this time them New York pitchers would know better than to give that guy anything he can hit.

In their part o' the ninth the Chief still had 'em shut out and two down, and the crowd was goin' home; but Doyle gets hit in the sleeve with a pitched ball and it's Speed's turn. He hits a foul pretty near straight up, but Schang misjudges it. Then he lifts another one and this time McInnes drops it. He'd ought to of been out twice. The Chief tries to make him hit at a bad one then, because he'd got him two strikes and nothin'. He hit at it all right—kissed it for three bases between Strunk and Joyce! And it was a wild pitch that he hit. Doyle scores, o' course, and the bugs suddenly decide not to go home just yet. I fully expected to see him steal home and get away with it, but Murray cut into the first ball and lined out to Barry.

Plank beat Matty two to one the next day in New York, and again Speed and his rabbit's foot give us an awful argument. Matty wasn't so good as usual and we really ought to of beat him bad. Two different times Strunk was on second waitin' for any kind o' wallop, and both times Barry cracked 'em down the third-base line like a shot. Speed stopped the first one with his stomach and extricated the pill just in time to nail Barry at first base and retire the side. The next time he throwed his glove in front of his face in self-defense and the ball stuck in it.

In the sixth innin' Schang was on third base and Plank on first, and two down, and Murphy combed an awful one to Speed's left. He didn't have time to stoop over and he just stuck out his foot. The ball hit it and caromed in two hops right into Doyle's hands on second base before Plank got there. Then in the seventh Speed bunts one and Baker trips and falls goin' after it or he'd of threw him out a mile. They was two gone; so Speed steals second, and, o' course, Schang has to make a bad peg right at that time and lets him go to third. Then Collins boots one on Murray and they've got a run. But it didn't do 'em no good, because Collins and Baker and McInnes come up in the ninth and walloped 'em where Parker couldn't reach 'em.

Comin' back to Philly on the train that night, I says to Connie:

"What do you think o' that Parker bird now?"

"He's lucky, all right," says Connie smilin'; "but we won't hold it against him if he don't beat us with it."

"It ain't too late," I says. "He ain't pulled his real stuff yet."

The whole bunch was talkin' about him and his luck, and sayin' it was about time for things to break against him. I warned 'em that they wasn't no chance—that it was permanent with him.

Bush and Tesreau hooked up next day and neither o' them had much stuff. Everybody was hittin' and it looked like anybody's game right up to the ninth. Speed had got on every time he come up—the wind blowin' his fly balls away from the outfielders and the infielders bootin' when he hit 'em on the ground.

When the ninth started the score was seven apiece. Connie and McGraw both had their whole pitchin' staffs warmin' up. The crowd was wild, because they'd been all kinds of action. They wasn't no danger of anybody's leavin' their seats before this game was over.

Well, Bescher is walked to start with and Connie's about ready to give Bush the hook; but Doyle pops out tryin' to bunt. Then Speed gets two strikes and two balls, and it looked to me like the next one was right over the heart; but Connolly calls it a ball and gives him another chance. He whales the groove ball to the fence in left center and gets round to third on it, while Bescher scores. Right then Bush comes out and the Chief goes in. He whiffs Murray and has two strikes on Merkle when Speed makes a break for home—and, o' course, that was the one ball Schang dropped in the whole serious!

They had a two-run lead on us then and it looked like a cinch for them to hold it, because the minute Tesreau showed a sign o' weakenin' McGraw was sure to holler for Matty or the Rube. But you know how quick that bunch of ourn can make a two-run lead look sick. Before McGraw could get Jeff out o' there we had two on the bases.

Then Rube comes in and fills 'em up by walkin' Joyce. It was Eddie's turn to wallop and if he didn't do nothin' we had Baker comin' up next. This time Collins saved Baker the trouble and whanged one clear to the woods. Everybody scored but him— and he could of, too, if it'd been necessary.

In the clubhouse the boys naturally felt pretty good. We'd copped three in a row and it looked like we'd make it four straight, because we had the Chief to send back at 'em the followin' day.

"Your friend Parker is lucky," the boys says to me, "but it don't look like he could stop us now."

I felt the same way and was consultin' the time-tables to see whether I could get a train out o' New York for the West next evenin'. But do you think Speed's luck was ready to quit? Not yet! And it's a wonder we didn't all go nuts durin' the next few days. If words could kill, Speed would of died a thousand times. And I wish he had!

They wasn't no record-breakin' crowd out when we got to the Polo Grounds. I guess the New York bugs was pretty well discouraged and the bettin' was eight to five that we'd cop that battle and finish it. The Chief was the only guy that warmed up for us and McGraw didn't have no choice but to use Matty, with the whole thing dependin' on this game.

They went along like the two swell pitchers they was till Speed's innin', which in this battle was the eighth. Nobody scored, and it didn't look like they was ever goin' to till Murphy starts off that round with a perfect bunt and Joyce sacrifices him to second. All Matty had to do then was to get rid o' Collins and Baker—and that's about as easy as sellin' silk socks to an Eskimo.

He didn't give Eddie nothin' he wanted to hit, though; and finally he slaps one on the ground to Doyle. Larry made the play to first base and Murphy moved to third. We all figured Matty'd walk Baker then, and he done it. Connie sends Baker down to second on the first pitch to McInnes, but Meyers don't pay no attention to him—they was playin' for McInnes and wasn't takin' no chances o' throwin' the ball away.

Well, the count goes to three and two on McInnes and Matty comes with a curve—he's got some curve too; but Jack happened to meet it and—Blooie! Down the left foul line where he always hits! I never seen a ball hit so hard in my life. No infielder in the world could of stopped it. But I'll give you a thousand bucks if that ball didn't go kerplunk right into the third bag and stop as dead as George Washington! It was child's play for Speed to pick it up and heave it over to Merkle before Jack got there. If anybody else had been playin' third base the bag would of ducked out o' the way o' that wallop; but even the bases themselves was helpin' him out.

The two runs we ought to of had on Jack's smash would of been just enough to beat 'em, because they got the only run o' the game in their half—or, I should say, the Lord give it to 'em.

Doyle's been throwed out and up come Parker, smilin'. The minute I seen him smile I felt like somethin' was comin' off and I made the remark on the bench.

Well, the Chief pitched one right at him and he tried to duck. The ball hit his bat and went on a line between Jack and Eddie. Speed didn't know he'd hit it till the guys on the bench wised him up. Then he just had time to get to first base. They tried the hit-and-run on the second ball and Murray lifts a high fly that Murphy didn't have to move for. Collins pulled the old bluff about the ball bein' on the ground and Barry yells, "Go on! Go on!" like he was the coacher. Speed fell for it and didn't know where the ball was no more'n a rabbit; he just run his fool head off and we was gettin' all ready to laugh when the ball come down and Murphy dropped it!

If Parker had stuck near first base, like he ought to of done, he couldn't of got no farther'n second; but with the start he got he was pretty near third when Murphy made the muff, and it was a cinch for him to score. The next two guys was easy outs; so they wouldn't of had a run except for Speed's boner. We couldn't do nothin' in the ninth and we was licked.

Well, that was a tough one to lose; but we figured that Matty was through and we'd wind it up the next day, as we had Plank ready to send back at 'em. We wasn't afraid o' the Rube, because he hadn't never bothered Collins and Baker much.

The two lefthanders come together just like everybody's doped it and it was about even up to the eighth. Plank had been goin' great and, though the score was two and two, they'd got their two on boots and we'd hit ourn in. We went after Rube in our part o' the eighth and knocked him out. Demaree stopped us after we'd scored two more.

"It's all over but the shoutin'!" says Davis on the bench.

"Yes," I says, "unless that seventh son of a seventh son gets up there again."

He did, and he come up after they'd filled the bases with a boot, a base hit and a walk with two out. I says to Davis:

"If I was Plank I'd pass him and give 'em one run."

"That wouldn't be no baseball," says Davis—"not with Murray comin' up."

Well, it mayn't of been no baseball, but it couldn't of turned out worse if they'd did it that way. Speed took a healthy at the first ball; but it was a hook and he caught it on the handle, right up near his hands. It started outside the first-base line like a foul and then changed its mind and rolled in. Schang run away from the plate, because it looked like it was up to him to make the play. He picked the ball up and had to make the peg in a hurry.

His throw hit Speed right on top o' the head and bounded off like it had struck a cement sidewalk. It went clear over to the seats and before McInnes could get it three guys had scored and Speed was on third base. He was left there, but that didn't make no difference. We was licked again and for the first time the gang really begun to get scared.

We went over to New York Sunday afternoon and we didn't do no singin' on the way. Some o' the fellers tried to laugh, but it hurt 'em. Connie sent us to bed early, but I don't believe none o' the bunch got much sleep—I know I didn't; I was worryin' too much about the serious and also about the girl, who hadn't sent me no telegram like I'd ast her to. Monday mornin' I wired her askin' what was the matter and tellin' her I was gettin' tired of her foolishness. O' course I didn't make it so strong as that—but the telegram cost me a dollar and forty cents.

Connie had the choice o' two pitchers for the sixth game. He could use Bush, who'd been slammed round pretty hard last time out, or the Chief, who'd only had two days' rest. The rest of 'em—outside o' Plank—had a epidemic o' sore arms. Connie finally picked Bush, so's he could have the Chief in reserve in case we had to play a seventh game. McGraw started Big Jeff and we went at it.

It wasn't like the last time these two guys had hooked up. This time they both had somethin', and for eight innin's runs was as scarce as Chinese policemen. They'd been chances to score on both sides, but the big guy and Bush was both tight in the pinches. The crowd was plumb nuts and yelled like Indians every time a fly ball was caught or a strike called. They'd of got their money's worth if they hadn't been no ninth; but, believe me, that was some round!

They was one out when Barry hit one through the box for a base. Schang walked, and it was Bush's turn. Connie told him to bunt, but he whiffed in the attempt. Then Murphy comes up and walks—and the bases are choked. Young Joyce had been pie for Tesreau all day or else McGraw might of changed pitchers right there. Anyway he left Big Jeff in and he beaned Joyce with a fast one. It sounded like a tire blowin' out. Joyce falls over in a heap and we chase out there, thinkin' he's dead; but he ain't, and pretty soon he gets up and walks down to first base. Tesreau had forced in a run and again we begun to count the winner's end. Matty comes in to prevent further damage and Collins flies the side out.

"Hold 'em now! Work hard!" we says to young Bush, and he walks out there just as cool as though he was goin' to hit fungoes.

McGraw sends up a pinch hitter for Matty and Bush whiffed him. Then Bescher flied out. I ws prayin' that Doyle would end it, because Speed's turn come after his'n; so I pretty near fell dead when Larry hit safe.

Speed had his old smile and even more chest than usual when he come up there, swingin' five or six bats. He didn't wait for

Doyle to try and steal, or nothin'. He lit into the first ball, though Bush was tryin' to waste it. I seen the ball go high in the air toward left field, and then I picked up my glove and got ready to beat it for the gate. But when I looked out to see if Joyce was set, what do you think I seen? He was lyin' flat on the ground! That blow on the head had got him just as Bush was pitchin' to Speed. He'd flopped over and didn't no more know what was goin' on than if he'd croaked.

Well, everybody else seen it at the same time; but it was too late. Strunk made a run for the ball, but they wasn't no chance for him to get near it. It hit the ground about ten feet back o' where Joyce was lyin' and bounded way over to the end o' the foul line. You don't have to be told that Doyle and Parker both scored and the serious was tied up.

We carried Joyce to the clubhouse and after a while he come to. He cried when he found out what had happened. We cheered him up all we could, but he was a pretty sick guy. The trainer said he'd be all right, though, for the final game.

They tossed up a coin to see where they'd play the seventh battle and our club won the toss; so we went back to Philly that night and cussed Parker clear across New Jersey. I was so sore I kicked the stuffin' out o' my seat.

You probably heard about the excitement in the burg yesterday mornin'. The demand for tickets was somethin' fierce and some of 'em sold for as high as twenty-five bucks apiece. Our club hadn't been lookin' for no seventh game and they was some tall hustlin' done round that old ball park.

I started out to the grounds early and bought some New York papers to read on the car. They was a big story that Speed Parker, the Giants' hero, was goin' to be married a week after the end o' the serious. It didn't give the name o' the girl, sayin' Speed had refused to tell it. I figured she must be some dame he'd met round the circuit somewheres.

They was another story by one o' them smart baseball reporters sayin' that Parker, on his way up to the plate, had saw that Joyce was about ready to faint and had hit the fly ball to left field on purpose. Can you beat it?

I was goin' to show that to the boys in the clubhouse, but the minute I blowed in there I got some news that made me forget about everything else. Joyce was very sick and they'd took him to a hospital. It was up to me to play!

Connie come over and ast me whether I'd ever hit against Matty. I told him I hadn't, but I'd saw enough of him to know he wasn't no worse'n Johnson. He told me he was goin' to let me hit second—in Joyce's place—because he didn't want to bust up the rest of his combination. He also told me to take my orders from Strunk about where to play for the batters.

"Where shall I play for Parker?" I says, tryin' to joke and pretend I wasn't scared to death.

"I wisht I could tell you," says Connie. "I guess the only thing to do when he comes up is to get down on your knees and pray."

The rest o' the bunch slapped me on the back and give me all the encouragement they could. The place was jammed when we went out on the field. They may of been bigger crowds before, but they never was packed together so tight. I doubt whether they was even room enough left for Falkenberg to sit down.

The afternoon papers had printed the stuff about Joyce bein' out of it, so the bugs was wise that I was goin' to play. They watched me pretty close in battin' practice and give me a hand whenever I managed to hit one hard. When I was out catchin' fungoes the guys in the bleachers cheered me and told me they was with me; but I don't mind tellin' you that I was as nervous as a bride.

They wasn't no need for the announcers to tip the crowd off to the pitchers. Everybody in the United States and Cuba knowed that the Chief'd work for us and Matty for them. The Chief didn't have no trouble with 'em in the first innin'. Even from where I stood I could see that he had a lot o' stuff. Bescher and Doyle popped out and Speed whiffed.

Well, I started out makin' good, with reverse English, in our part. Fletcher booted Murphy's ground ball and I was sent up to sacrifice. I done a complete job of it—sacrificin' not only myself but Murphy with a pop fly that Matty didn't have to move for. That spoiled whatever chance we had o' gettin' the jump on 'em; but the boys didn't bawl me for it.

"That's all right, old boy. You're all right!" they said on the bench—if they'd had a gun they'd of shot me.

I didn't drop no fly balls in the first six innin's—because none was hit out my way. The Chief was so good that they wasn't hittin' nothin' out o' the infield. And we wasn't doin' nothin' with Matty, either. I led off in the fourth and fouled the first one. I didn't molest the other two. But if Connie and the gang talked about me they done it internally. I come up again—with Murphy on third base and two gone in the sixth, and done my little whiffin' specialty. And still the only people that panned me was the thirty thousand that had paid for the privilege!

My first fieldin' chance come in the seventh. You'd of thought that I'd of had my nerve back by that time; but I was just as scared as though I'd never saw a crowd before. It was just as well that they was two out when Merkle hit one to me. I staggered under it and finally it hit me on the shoulder. Merkle got to second, but the Chief whiffed the next guy. I was gave some cross looks on the bench and I shouldn't of blamed the fellers if they'd cut loose with some language; but they didn't.

They's no use in me tellin' you about none o' the rest of it—except what happened just before the start o' the eleventh and durin' that innin', which was sure the big one o' yesterday's pastime—both for Speed and yours sincerely.

The scoreboard was still a row o' ciphers and Speed'd had only a fair amount o' luck. He'd made a scratch base hit and robbed our bunch of a couple o' real ones with impossible stops.

When Schang flied out and wound up our tenth I was leanin' against the end of our bench. I heard my name spoke, and I turned round and seen a boy at the door.

"Right here!" I says; and he give me a telegram.

"Better not open it till after the game," says Connie.

"Oh, no; it ain't no bad news," I said, for I figured it was an answer from the girl. So I opened it up and read it on the way to my position. It said:

"Forgive me, Dick—and forgive Speed too. Letter follows."

Well, sir, I ain't no baby, but for a minute I just wanted to sit down and bawl. And then, all of a sudden, I got so mad I couldn't see. I run right into Baker as he was pickin' up his glove. Then I give him a shove and called him some name, and him and Barry both looked at me like I was crazy—and I was. When I got out in left field I stepped on my own foot and spiked it. I just had to hurt somebody.

As I remember it the Chief fanned the first two of 'em. Then Doyle catches one just right and lams it up against the fence back o' Murphy. The ball caromed round some and Doyle got all the way to third base. Next thing I seen was Speed struttin' up to the plate. I run clear in from my position.

"Kill him!" I says to the Chief. "Hit him in the head and kill him, and I'll go to jail for it!"

"Are you off your nut?" says the Chief. "Go out there and play ball—and quit ravin'."

Barry and Baker led me away and give me a shove out toward left. Then I heard the crack o' the bat and I seen the ball comin' a mile a minute. It was headed between Strunk and I and looked like it would go out o' the park. I don't remember runnin' or nothin' about it till I run into the concrete wall head first. They told me afterward and all the papers said that it was the greatest catch ever seen. And I never knowed I'd caught the ball!

Some o' the managers have said my head was pretty hard, but it wasn't as hard as that concrete. I was pretty near out, but they tell me I walked to the bench like I wasn't hurt at all. They also tell me that the crowd was a bunch o' ravin' maniacs and was throwin' money at me. I guess the ground-keeper'll get it.

The boys on the bench was all talkin' at once and slappin' me on the back, but I didn't know what it was about. Somebody told me pretty soon that it was my turn to hit and I picked up the first bat I come to and starts for the plate. McInnes comes runnin' after me and ast me whether I didn't want my own bat. I cussed him and told him to mind his own business.

I didn't know it at the time, but I found out afterward that they was two out. The bases was empty. I'll tell you just what I had in my mind: I wasn't thinkin' about the ball game; I was determined that I was goin' to get to third base and give that guy my spikes. If I didn't hit one worth three bases, or if I didn't hit one at all, I was goin' to run till I got round to where Speed was, and then slide into him and cut him to pieces!

Right now I can't tell you whether I hit a fast ball, or a slow ball, or a hook, or a fader—but I hit somethin'. It went over Bescher's head like a shot and then took a crazy bound. It must of struck a rock or a pop bottle, because it hopped clear over the fence and landed in the bleachers.

Mind you, I learned this afterward. At the time I just knowed I'd hit one somewheres and I starts round the bases. I speeded up when I got near third and took a runnin' jump at a guy I thought was Parker. I missed him and sprawled all over the bag. Then, all of a sudden, I come to my senses. All the Ath-a-letics was out there to run home with me and it was one o' them I'd tried to cut. Speed had left the field. The boys picked me up and seen to it that I went on and touched the plate. Then I was carried into the clubhouse by the crazy bugs.

Well, they had a celebration in there and it was a long time before I got a chance to change my clothes. The boys made a big fuss over me. They told me they'd intended to give me five hundred bucks for my divvy, but now I was goin' to get a full share.

"Parker ain't the only lucky guy!" says one of 'em. "But even if that ball hadn't of took that crazy hop you'd of had a triple."

A triple! That's just what I'd wanted; and he called me lucky for not gettin' it!

The Giants was dressin' in the other part o' the clubhouse; and when I finally come out there was Speed, standin' waitin' for some o' the others. He seen me comin' and he smiled. "Hello, Horseshoes!" he says.

He won't smile no more for a while—it'll hurt too much. And if any girl wants him when she sees him now—with his nose over shakin' hands with his ear, and his jaw a couple o' feet foul—she's welcome to him. They won't be no contest!

Grimes leaned over to ring for the waiter.

"Well," he said, "what about it?"

"You won't have to pay my fare," I told him.

"I'll buy a drink anyway," said he. "You've been a good listener—and I had to get it off my chest."

"Maybe they'll have to postpone the wedding," I said.

"No," said Grimes. "The weddin' will take place the day after tomorrow—and I'll bat for Mr. Parker. Did you think I was goin' to let him get away with it?"

"What about next year?" I asked.

"I'm going back to the Ath-a-letics," he said. "And I'm goin' to hire somebody to call me 'Horseshoes!' before every game—because I can sure play that old baseball when I'm mad."

SOME LIKE THEM COLD

N. Y., Aug. 3.

Dear Miss Gillespie:

How about our bet now as you bet me I would forget all about you the minute I hit the big town and would never write you a letter. Well girlie it looks like you lose so pay me. Seriously we will call all bets off as I am not the kind that bet on a sure thing and it sure was a sure thing that I would not forget a girlie like you and all that is worrying me is whether it may not be the other way round and you are wondering who this fresh guy is that is writeing you this letter. I bet you are so will try and re-freshen your memory.

Well girlie I am the handsome young man that was wondering round the Lasalle st. station Monday and "happened" to sit down beside of a mighty pretty girlie who was waiting to meet her sister from Toledo and the train was late and I am glad of it be-cause if it had not of been that little girlie and I would never of met. So for once I was a lucky guy but still I guess it was time I had some luck as it was certainly tough luck for you and I to both be liveing in Chi all that time and never get together till a half hour before I was leaving town for good.

Still "better late than never" you know and maybe we can make up for lost time though it looks like we would have to do our makeing up at long distants unless you make good on your threat and come to N. Y. I wish you would do that little thing girlie as it looks like that was the only way we would get a chance to play round together as it looks like they was little or no chance of me comeing back to Chi as my whole future is in the big town. N. Y. is the only spot and specially for a man that expects to make my liveing in the song writeing game as here is the Mecca for that line of work and no matter how good a man may be they don't get no recognition unless they live in N. Y.

Well girlie you asked me to tell you all about my trip. Well I remember you saying that you would give anything to be makeing it yourself but as far as the trip itself was conserned you ought to be thankfull you did not have to make it as you would of sweat your head off. I know I did specially wile going through Ind. Monday P.M. But Monday night was the worst of all trying to sleep and finely I give it up and just layed there with the prespiration rolling off of me though I was laying on top of the covers and nothing on but my underwear.

Yesterday was not so bad as it rained most of the A.M. comeing through N. Y. state and in the P.M. we road along side of the Hudson all P.M. Some river girlie and just looking at it makes a man forget all about the heat and everything else except a certain girlie who I seen for the first time Monday and then only for a half hour but she is the kind of a girlie that a man don't need to see her only once and they would be no danger of forgetting her. There I guess I better lay off that subject or you will think I am a "fresh guy."

Well that is about all to tell you about the trip only they was one amuseing incidence that come off yesterday which I will tell you. Well they was a dame got on the train at Toledo Monday and had the birth opp. mine but I did not see nothing of her that night as I was out smoking till late and she hit the hay early but yesterday A.M. she come in the dinner and sit at the same table with me and tried to make me and it was so raw that the dinge waiter seen it and give me the wink and of course I paid no tension and I waited till she got through so as they would be no danger of her folling me out but she stopped on the way out to get a tooth pick and when I come out she was out on the platform with it so I tried to brush right by but she spoke up and asked me what time it was and I told her and she said she geussed her watch was slow so I said maybe it just seemed slow on acct. of the company it was in.

I don't know if she got what I was driveing at or not but any way she give up trying to make me and got off at Albany. She was a good looker but I have no time for gals that trics to make strangers on a train.

Well if I don't quit you will think I am writeing a book but will expect a long letter in answer to this letter and we will see if you can keep your promise like I have kept mine. Don't dissapoint me girlie as I am all alone in a large city and hearing from you will keep me from getting home sick for old Chi though I never thought so much of the old town till I found out you lived there. Don't think that is kidding girlie as I mean it.

You can address me at this hotel as it looks like I will be here right along as it is on 47th st. right off of old Broadway and handy to everything and am only paying $21 per wk. for my rm. and could of got one for $16 but without bath but am glad to pay the difference as am lost without my bath in the A.M. and sometimes at night too.

Tomorrow I expect to commence fighting the "battle of Broadway" and will let you know how I come out that is if you answer this letter. In the mean wile girlie au reservoir and don't do nothing I would not do.

Your new friend (?)
CHAS. F. LEWIS.

Chicago, Ill., Aug. 6.

My Dear Mr. Lewis:

Well, that certainly was a "surprise party" getting your letter and you are certainly a "wonder man" to keep your word as I am afraid most men of your sex are gay deceivers but maybe you are "different." Any way it sure was a surprise and will gladly pay the bet if you will just tell me what it was we bet. Hope it was not money as I am a "working girl" but if it was not more than a dollar or two will try to dig it up even if I have to "beg, borrow or steal."

Suppose you will think me a "case" to make a bet and then forget what it was, but you must remember, Mr. Man, that I had just met you and was "dazzled." Joking aside I was rather "fussed" and will tell you why. Well, Mr. Lewis, I suppose you see lots of girls like the one you told me about that you saw on the train who tried to "get acquainted" but I want to assure you that I am not one of those kind and sincerely hope you will believe me when I tell you that you was the first man I ever spoke to meeting them like that and my friends and the people who know me would simply faint if they knew I ever spoke to a man without a "proper introduction."

Believe me, Mr. Lewis, I am not that kind and I don't know now why I did it only that you was so "different" looking if you know what I mean and not at all like the kind of men that usually try to force their attentions on every pretty girl they see. Lots of times I act on impulse and let my feelings run away from me and sometimes I do things on the impulse of the moment which I regret them later on, and that is what I did this time, but hope you won't give me cause to regret it and I know you won't as I know you are not that kind of a man a specially after what you told me about the girl on the train. But any way as I say, I was in a "daze" so can't remember what it was we bet, but will try and pay it if it does not "break" me.

Sis's train got in about ten minutes after yours had gone and when she saw me what do you think was the first thing she said? Well, Mr. Lewis, she said: "Why Mibs (That is a pet name some of my friends have given me) what has happened to you? I never seen you have as much color." So I passed it off with some re-

mark about the heat and changed the subject as I certainly was
not going to tell her that I had just been talking to a man who I
had never met or she would of dropped dead from the shock.
Either that or she would not of believed me as it would be hard
for a person who knows me well to imagine me doing a thing
like that as I have quite a reputation for "squelching" men who
try to act fresh. I don't mean anything personal by that, Mr.
Lewis, as am a good judge of character and could tell without
you telling me that you are not that kind.

Well, Sis and I have been on the "go" ever since she arrived
as I took yesterday and today off so I could show her the "sights"
though she says she would be perfectly satisfied to just sit in the
apartment and listen to me "rattle on." Am afraid I am a great
talker, Mr. Lewis, but Sis says it is as good as a show to hear me
talk as I tell things in such a different way as I cannot help from
seeing the humorous side of everything and she says she never
gets tired of listening to me, but of course she is my sister and
thinks the world of me, but she really does laugh like she enjoyed
my craziness.

Maybe I told you that I have a tiny apartment which a girl
friend of mine and I have together and it is hardly big enough
to turn round in, but still it is "home" and I am a great home girl
and hardly ever care to go out evenings except occasionally to
the theatre or dance. But even if our "nest" is small we are proud
of it and Sis complimented us on how cozy it is and how "homey"
it looks and she said she did not see how we could afford to have
everything so nice and Edith (my girl friend) said: "Mibs de-
serves all the credit for that. I never knew a girl who could make
a little money go a long ways like she can." Well, of course she
is my best friend and always saying nice things about me, but I
do try and I hope I get results. Have always said that good taste
and being careful is a whole lot more important than lots of
money though it is nice to have it.

You must write and tell me how you are getting along in the

"battle of Broadway" (I laughed when I read that) and whether
the publishers like your songs though I know they will. Am
crazy to hear them and hear you play the piano as I love good
jazz music even better than classical, though I suppose it is terrible to say such a thing. But I usually say just what I think
though sometimes I wish afterwards I had not of. But still I
believe it is better for a girl to be her own self and natural instead of always acting. But am afraid I will never have a chance
to hear you play unless you come back to Chi and pay us a visit
as my "threat" to come to New York was just a "threat" and I
don't see any hope of ever getting there unless some rich New
Yorker should fall in love with me and take me there to live. Fine
chance for poor little me, eh Mr. Lewis?

Well, I guess I have "rattled on" long enough and you will think
I am writing a book unless I quit and besides, Sis has asked me as
a special favor to make her a pie for dinner. Maybe you don't
know it, Mr. Man, but I am quite famous for my pie and pastry,
but I don't suppose a "genius" is interested in common things
like that.

Well, be sure and write soon and tell me what N. Y. is like and
all about it and don't forget the little girlie who was "bad" and
spoke to a strange man in the station and have been blushing over
it ever since.

Your friend (?)
MABELLE GILLESPIE.

N. Y., Aug. 10.

Dear Girlie:

I bet you will think I am a fresh guy commenceing that way
but Miss Gillespie is too cold and a man can not do nothing cold
in this kind of weather specially in this man's town which is the
hottest place I ever been in and I guess maybe the reason why

New Yorkers is so bad is because they think they are all ready
in H—— and can not go no worse place no matter how they be-
have themselves. Honest girlie I certainly envy you being where
there is a breeze off the old Lake and Chi may be dirty but I
never heard of nobody dying because they was dirty but four
people died here yesterday on acct. of the heat and I seen two different women flop right on Broadway and had to be taken away
in the ambulance and it could not of been because they were
dressed too warm because it would be impossible for the women
here to leave off any more cloths.

Well have not had much luck yet in the battle of Broadway
as all the heads of the big music publishers is out of town on their
vacation and the big boys is the only ones I will do business with
as it would be silly for a man with the stuff I have got to waste
my time on somebody that is just on the staff and have not got
the final say. But I did play a couple of my numbers for the people up to Levy's and Goebel's and they went crazy over them
in both places. So it looks like all I have to do is wait for the big
boys to get back and then play my numbers for them and I will
be all set. What I want is to get taken on the staff of one of the
big firms as that gives a man the inside and they will plug your
numbers more if you are on the staff. In the mean wile have not
got nothing to worry me but am just seeing the sights of the big
town as have saved up enough money to play round for a wile
and any way a man that can play piano like I can don't ever have
to worry about starveing. Can certainly make the old music box
talk girlie and am always good for a $75 or $100 job.

Well have been here a week now and on the go every minute
and I thought I would be lonesome down here but no chance of
that as I have been treated fine by the people I have met and have
sure met a bunch of them. One of the boys liveing in the hotel
is a vaudeville actor and he is a member of the Friars club and
took me over there to dinner the other night and some way an-

other the bunch got wise that I could play piano so of course I had to sit down and give them some of my numbers and everybody went crazy over them. One of the boys I met there was Paul Sears the song writer but he just writes the lyrics and has wrote a bunch of hits and when he heard some of my melodies he called me over to one side and said he would like to work with me on some numbers. How is that girlie as he is one of the biggest hit writers in N. Y.

N. Y. has got some mighty pretty girlies and I guess it would not be hard to get acquainted with them and in fact several of them has tried to make me since I been here but I always figure that a girl must be something wrong with her if she tries to make a man that she don't know nothing about so I pass them all up. But I did meet a couple of pips that a man here in the hotel went up on Riverside Drive to see them and insisted on me going along and they got on some way that I could make a piano talk so they was nothing but I must play for them so I sit down and played some of my own stuff and they went crazy over it.

One of the girls wanted I should come up and see her again, and I said I might but I think I better keep away as she acted like she wanted to vamp me and I am not the kind that likes to play round with a gal just for their company and dance with them etc. but when I see the right gal that will be a different thing and she won't have to beg me to come and see her as I will camp right on her trail till she says yes. And it won't be none of these N. Y. fly by nights either. They are all right to look at but a man would be a sucker to get serious with them as they might take you up and next thing you know you would have a wife on your hands that don't know a dish rag from a waffle iron.

Well girlie will quit and call it a day as it is too hot to write any more and I guess I will turn on the cold water and lay in the tub a wile and then turn in. Don't forget to write to

Your friend,
CHAS. F. LEWIS.

Dear Mr. Man:

Hope you won't think me a "silly Billy" for starting my letter that way but "Mr. Lewis" is so formal and "Charles" is too much the other way and any way I would not dare call a man by their first name after only knowing them only two weeks. Though I may as well confess that Charles is my favorite name for a man and have always been crazy about it as it was my father's name. Poor old dad, he died of cancer three years ago, but left enough insurance so that mother and we girls were well provided for and do not have to do anything to support ourselves though I have been earning my own living for two years to make things easier for mother and also because I simply can't bear to be doing nothing as I feel like a "drone." So I flew away from the "home nest" though mother felt bad about it as I was her favorite and she always said I was such a comfort to her as when I was in the house she never had to worry about how things would go.

But there I go gossiping about my domestic affairs just like you would be interested in them though I don't see how you could be though personaly I always like to know all about my friends, but I know men are different so will try and not bore you any longer. Poor Man, I certainly feel sorry for you if New York is as hot as all that. I guess it has been very hot in Chi, too, at least everybody has been complaining about how terrible it is. Suppose you will wonder why I say "I guess" and you will think I ought to know if it is hot. Well, sir, the reason I say "I guess" is because I don't feel the heat like others do or at least I don't let myself feel it. That sounds crazy I know, but don't you think there is a good deal in mental suggestion and not letting yourself feel things? I believe that if a person simply won't allow themselves to be affected by disagreeable things, why such things won't bother them near as much. I know it works with me and that is the reason why I am never cross when things go wrong and "keep smiling" no matter what happens and as far as the heat is concerned, why I just don't let myself feel it and my friends say I don't even look hot no matter if the weather is boiling and Edith, my girl friend, often says that I am like a breeze and it cools her off just to have me come in the room. Poor Edie suffers terribly during the hot weather and says it almost makes her mad at me to see how cool and unruffled I look when everybody else is perspiring and have red faces etc.

I laughed when I read what you said about New York being so hot that people thought it was the "other place." I can appreciate a joke, Mr. Man, and that one did not go "over my head." Am still laughing at some of the things you said in the station though they probably struck me funnier than they would most girls as I always see the funny side and sometimes something is said and I laugh and the others wonder what I am laughing at as they cannot see anything in it themselves, but it is just the way I look at things so of course I cannot explain to them why I laughed and they think I am crazy. But I had rather part with almost anything rather than my sense of humour as it helps me over a great many rough spots.

Sis has gone back home though I would of liked to of kept her here much longer, but she had to go though she said she would of liked nothing better than to stay with me and just listen to me "rattle on." She always says it is just like a show to hear me talk as I always put things in such a funny way and for weeks after she has been visiting me she thinks of some of the things I said and laughs over them. Since she left Edith and I have been pretty quiet though poor Edie wants to be on the "go" all the time and tries to make me go out with her every evening to the pictures and scolds me when I say I had rather stay home and read and calls me a "book worm." Well, it is true that I had rather stay home with a good book than go to some crazy old picture and the last two nights I have been reading myself to sleep with

Robert W. Service's poems. Don't you love Service or don't you care for "highbrow" writings?

Personly there is nothing I love more than to just sit and read a good book or sit and listen to somebody play the piano, I mean if they can really play and I really believe I like popular music better than the classical though I suppose that is a terrible thing to confess, but I love all kinds of music but a specially the piano when it is played by somebody who can really play.

Am glad you have not "fallen" for the "ladies" who have tried to make your acquaintance in New York. You are right in thinking there must be something wrong with girls who try to "pick up" strange men as no girl with self respect would do such a thing and when I say that, Mr. Man, I know you will think it is a funny thing for me to say on account of the way our friendship started, but I mean it and I assure you that was the first time I ever done such a thing in my life and would never of thought of doing it had I not known you were the right kind of a man as I flatter myself that I am a good judge of character and can tell pretty well what a person is like by just looking at them and I assure you I had made up my mind what kind of a man you were before I allowed myself to answer your opening remark. Otherwise I am the last girl in the world that would allow myself to speak to a person without being introduced to them.

When you write again you must tell me all about the girl on Riverside Drive and what she looks like and if you went to see her again and all about her. Suppose you will think I am a little old "curiosity shop" for asking all those questions and will wonder why I want to know. Well, sir, I won't tell you why, so there, but I insist on you answering all questions and will scold you if you don't. Maybe you will think that the reason why I am so curious is because I am "jealous" of the lady in question. Well, sir, I won't tell you whether I am or not, but will keep you "guessing." Now, don't you wish you knew?

Must close or you will think I am going to "rattle on" forever or maybe you have all ready become disgusted and torn my letter up. If so all I can say is poor little me—she was a nice little girl and meant well, but the man did not appreciate her.

There! Will stop or you will think I am crazy if you do not all ready.

> *Yours* (?)
> MABELLE.

N. Y., Aug. 20.

Dear Girlie:

Well girlie I suppose you thought I was never going to answer your letter but have been busier than a one armed paper hanger the last week as have been working on a number with Paul Sears who is one of the best lyric writers in N. Y. and has turned out as many hits as Berlin or Davis or any of them. And believe me girlie he has turned out another hit this time that is he and I have done it together. It is all done now and we are just waiting for the best chance to place it but will not place it nowheres unless we get the right kind of a deal but maybe will publish it ourselves.

The song is bound to go over big as Sears has wrote a great lyric and I have give it a great tune or at least every body that has heard it goes crazy over it and it looks like it would go over bigger than any song since Mammy and would not be surprised to see it come out the hit of the year. If it is handled right we will make a bbl. of money and Sears says it is a cinch we will clean up as much as $25000 apiece which is pretty fair for one song but this one is not like the most of them but has got a great lyric and I have wrote a melody that will knock them out of their seats. I only wish you could hear it girlie and hear it the way I play it. I had to play it over and over about 50 times at the Friars last night.

I will copy down the lyric of the chorus so you can see what it is like and get the idea of the song though of course you can't tell much about it unless you hear it played and sang. The title of the song is When They're Like You and here is the chorus:

"*Some like them hot, some like them cold.*
Some like them when they're not too darn old.
Some like them fat, some like them lean.
Some like them only at sweet sixteen.
Some like them dark, some like them light.
Some like them in the park, late at night.
Some like them fickle, some like them true,
But the time I like them is when they're like you."

How is that for a lyric and I only wish I could play my melody for you as you would go nuts over it but will send you a copy as soon as the song is published and you can get some of your friends to play it over for you and I know you will like it though it is a different melody when I play it or when somebody else plays it.

Well girlie you will see how busy I have been and am libel to keep right on being busy as we are not going to let the grass grow under our feet but as soon as we have got this number placed we will get busy on another one as a couple like that will put me on Easy st. even if they don't go as big as we expect but even 25 grand is a big bunch of money and if a man could only turn out one hit a year and make that much out of it I would be on Easy st. and no more hammering on the old music box in some cabaret.

Who ever we take the song to we will make them come across with one grand for advance royaltys and that will keep me going till I can turn out another one. So the future looks bright and rosey to yours truly and I am certainly glad I come to the big town though sorry I did not do it a whole lot quicker.

This is a great old town girlie and when you have lived here a wile you wonder how you ever stood for a burg like Chi which is just a hick town along side of this besides being dirty etc. and a man is a sucker to stay there all his life specially a man in my line of work as N. Y. is the Mecca for a man that has got the musical gift. I figure that all the time I spent in Chi I was just wasteing my time and never really started to live till I come down here and I have to laugh when I think of the boys out there that is trying to make a liveing in the song writeing game and most of them starve to death all their life and the first week I am down here I meet a man like Sears and the next thing you know we have turned out a song that will make us a fortune.

Well girlie you asked me to tell you about the girlie up on the Drive that tried to make me and asked me to come and see her again. Well I can assure you you have no reasons to be jealous in that quarter as I have not been back to see her as I figure it is wasteing my time to play round with a dame like she that wants to go out somewheres every night and if you married her she would want a house on 5th ave. with a dozen servants so I have passed her up as that is not my idea of home.

What I want when I get married is a real home where a man can stay home and work and maybe have a few of his friends in once in a wile and entertain them or go to a good musical show once in a wile and have a wife that is in sympathy with you and not nag at you all the wile but be a real help mate. The girlie up on the Drive would run me ragged and have me in the poor house inside of a year even if I was makeing 25 grand out of one song. Besides she wears a make up that you would have to blast to find out what her face looks like. So I have not been back there and don't intend to see her again so what is the use of me telling you about her. And the only other girlie I have met is a sister of Paul Sears who I met up to his house wile we was working on the song but she don't hardly count as she has not got no use for the boys but treats them like dirt and Paul says she is the coldest proposition he ever seen.

Well I don't know no more to write and besides have got a date to go out to Paul's place for dinner and play some of my stuff for him so as he can see if he wants to set words to some more of my melodies. Well don't do nothing I would not do and have as good a time as you can in old Chi and will let you know how we come along with the song.

CHAS. F. LEWIS.

Chicago, Ill., Aug. 23.

Dear Mr. Man:

I am thrilled to death over the song and think the words awfully pretty and am crazy to hear the music which I know must be great. It must be wonderful to have the gift of writing songs and then hear people play and sing them and just think of making $25,000 in such a short time. My, how rich you will be and I certainly congratulate you though am afraid when you are rich and famous you will have no time for insignificant little me or will you be an exception and remember your "old" friends even when you are up in the world? I sincerely hope so.

Will look forward to receiving a copy of the song and will you be sure and put your name on it? I am all ready very conceited just to think that I know a man that writes songs and makes all that money.

Seriously I wish you success with your next song and I laughed when I read your remark about being busier than a one armed paper hanger. I don't see how you think up all those comparisons and crazy things to say. The next time one of the girls asks me to go out with them I am going to tell them I can't go because I am busier than a one armed paper hanger and then they will think I made it up and say: "The girl is clever."

Seriously I am glad you did not go back to see the girl on the Drive and am also glad you don't like girls who makes themselves up so much as I think it is disgusting and would rather go round looking like a ghost than put artificial color on my face. Fortunately I have a complexion that does not need "fixing" but even if my coloring was not what it is I would never think of lowering myself to "fix" it. But I must tell you a joke that happened just the other day when Edith and I were out at lunch and there was another girl in the restaurant whom Edie knew and she introduced her to me and I noticed how this girl kept staring at me and finally she begged my pardon and asked if she could ask me a personal question and I said yes and she asked me if my complexion was really "mine." I assured her it was and she said: "Well, I thought so because I did not think anybody could put it on so artistically. I certainly envy you." Edie and I both laughed.

Well, if that girl envies me my complexion, why I envy you living in New York. Chicago is rather dirty though I don't let that part of it bother me as I bathe and change my clothing so often that the dirt does not have time to "settle." Edie often says she cannot see how I always keep so clean looking and says I always look like I had just stepped out of a band box. She also calls me a fish (jokingly) because I spend so much time in the water. But seriously I do love to bathe and never feel so happy as when I have just "cleaned up" and put on fresh clothing.

Edie has just gone out to see a picture and was cross at me because I would not go with her. I told her I was going to write a letter and she wanted to know to whom and I told her and she said: "You write to him so often that a person would almost think you was in love with him." I just laughed and turned it off, but she does say the most embarrassing things and I would be angry if it was anybody but she that said them.

Seriously I had much rather sit here and write letters or read or just sit and dream than go out to some crazy old picture show except once in awhile I do like to go to the theater and see a good play and a specially a musical play if the music is catchy. But as a rule I am contented to just stay home and feel cozy and lots of evenings Edie and I sit here without saying hardly a word to each other though she would love to talk but she knows I had rather be quiet and she often says it is just like living with a deaf and dumb mute to live with me because I make so little noise round the apartment. I guess I was born to be a home body as I so seldom care to go "gadding."

Though I do love to have company once in awhile, just a few congenial friends whom I can talk to and feel at home with and play cards or have some music. My friends love to drop in here, too, as they say Edie and I always give them such nice things to eat. Though poor Edie has not much to do with it, I am afraid, as she hates anything connected with cooking which is one of the things I love best of anything and I often say that when I begin keeping house in my own home I will insist on doing most of my own work as I would take so much more interest in it than a servant, though I would want somebody to help me a little if I could afford it as I often think a woman that does all her own work is liable to get so tired that she loses interest in the bigger things of life like books and music. Though after all what bigger thing is there than home making a specially for a woman?

I am sitting in the dearest old chair that I bought yesterday at a little store on the North Side. That is my one extravagance, buying furniture and things for the house, but I always say it is economy in the long run as I will always have them and have use for them and when I can pick them up at a bargain I would be silly not to. Though heaven knows I will never be "poor" in regards to furniture and rugs and things like that as mother's house in Toledo is full of lovely things which she says she is going to give to Sis and myself as soon as we have real homes of our own. She is going to give me the first choice as I am her favorite. She has the loveliest old things that you could not buy now for love or money including lovely old rugs and a piano which Sis wanted to have a player attachment put on it but I said it would be an insult to the piano so we did not get one.

I am funny about things like that, a specially old furniture and feel towards them like people whom I love.

Poor mother, I am afraid she won't live much longer to enjoy her lovely old things as she has been suffering for years from stomach trouble and the doctor says it has been worse lately instead of better and her heart is weak besides. I am going home to see her a few days this fall as it may be the last time. She is very cheerful and always says she is ready to go now as she has had enough joy out of life and all she would like would be to see her girls settled down in their own homes before she goes.

There I go, talking about my domestic affairs again and I will bet you are bored to death though personly I am never bored when my friends tell me about themselves. But I won't "rattle on" any longer, but will say good night and don't forget to write and tell me how you come out with the song and thanks for sending me the words to it. Will you write a song about me some time? I would be thrilled to death! But I am afraid I am not the kind of girl that inspires men to write songs about them, but am just a quiet "mouse" that loves home and am not giddy enough to be the heroine of a song.

Well, Mr. Man, good night and don't wait so long before writing again to

Yours (?)
MABELLE.

Dear Girlie:

Well girlie have not got your last letter with me so cannot answer what was in it as I have forgotten if there was anything I was supposed to answer and besides have only a little time to write as I have a date to go out on a party with the Sears. We are going to the Georgie White show and afterwards somewheres for supper. Sears is the boy who wrote the lyric to my song and it is him and his sister I am going on the party with. The sister is a cold fish that has no use for men but she is show crazy and insists on Paul takeing her to 3 or 4 of them a week.

Paul wants me to give up my room here and come and live with them as they have plenty of room and I am running a little low on money but don't know if I will do it or not as am afraid I would freeze to death in the same house with a girl like the sister as she is ice cold but she don't hang round the house much as she is always takeing trips or going to shows or somewheres.

So far we have not had no luck with the song. All the publishers we have showed it to has went crazy over it but they won't make the right kind of a deal with us and if they don't loosen up and give us a decent royalty rate we are libel to put the song out ourselves and show them up. The man up to Goebel's told us the song was O. K. and he liked it but it was more of a production number than anything else and ought to go in a show like the Follies but they won't be in N. Y. much longer and what we ought to do is hold it till next spring.

Mean wile I am working on some new numbers and also have taken a position with the orchestra at the Wilton and am going to work there starting next week. They pay good money $60 and it will keep me going.

Well girlie that is about all the news. I believe you said your father was sick and hope he is better and also hope you are getting along O. K. and take care of yourself. When you have nothing else to do write to your friend,

CHAS. F. LEWIS.

Chicago, Ill., Sept. 11.

Dear Mr. Lewis:

Your short note reached me yesterday and must say I was puzzled when I read it. It sounded like you was mad at me though I cannot think of any reason why you should be. If there was something I said in my last letter that offended you I wish you would tell me what it was and I will ask your pardon though I cannot remember anything I could of said that you could take offense at. But if there was something, why I assure you, Mr. Lewis, that I did not mean anything by it. I certainly did not intend to offend you in any way.

Perhaps it is nothing I wrote you, but you are worried on account of the publishers not treating you fair in regards to your song and that is why your letter sounded so distant. If that is the case I hope that by this time matters have rectified themselves and the future looks brighter. But any way, Mr. Lewis, don't allow yourself to worry over business cares as they will all come right in the end and I always think it is silly for people to worry themselves sick over temporary troubles, but the best way is to "keep smiling" and look for the "silver lining" in the cloud. That is the way I always do and no matter what happens, I manage to smile and my girl friend, Edie, calls me Sunny because I always look on the bright side.

Remember also, Mr. Lewis, that $60 is a salary that a great many men would like to be getting and are living on less than that and supporting a wife and family on it. I always say that a person can get along on whatever amount they make if they manage things in the right way.

So if it is business troubles, Mr. Lewis, I say don't worry, but look on the bright side. But if it is something I wrote in my last letter that offended you I wish you would tell me what it was so I can apologize as I assure you I meant nothing and would not say anything to hurt you for the world.

Please let me hear from you soon as I will not feel comfortable until I know I am not to blame for the sudden change.

Sincerely,
MABELLE GILLESPIE.

N. Y. Sept. 24.

Dear Miss Gillespie:

Just a few lines to tell you the big news or at least it is big news to me. I am engaged to be married to Paul Sears' sister and we are going to be married early next month and live in Atlantic City where the orchestra I have been playing with has got an engagement in one of the big cabarets.

I know this will be a surprise to you as it was even a surprise to me as I did not think I would ever have the nerve to ask the girlie the big question as she was always so cold and acted like I was just in the way. But she said she supposed she would have to marry somebody some time and she did not dislike me as much as most of the other men her brother brought round and she would marry me with the understanding that she would not have to be a slave and work round the house and also I would have to take her to a show or somewheres every night and if I could not take her myself she would "run wild" alone. Atlantic City will be O. K. for that as a lot of new shows opens down there and she will be able to see them before they get to the big town. As for her being a slave, I would hate to think of marrying a girl and then have them spend their lives in druggery round the house. We are going to live in a hotel till we find something better but will be in no hurry to start house keeping as we will have to buy all new furniture.

Betsy is some doll when she is all fixed up and believe me she knows how to fix herself up. I don't know what she uses but it is weather proof and I have been out in a rain storm with her and we both got drowned but her face stayed on. I would almost think it was real only she tells me different.

Well girlie I may write to you again once in a wile as Betsy says she don't give a damn if I write to all the girls in the world just so I don't make her read the answers but that is all I can think of to say now except good bye and good luck and may the right man come along soon and he will be a lucky man getting a girl that is such a good cook and got all that furniture etc.

But just let me give you a word of advice before I close and that is don't never speak to strange men who you don't know nothing about as they may get you wrong and think you are trying to make them. It just happened that I knew better so you was lucky in my case but the luck might not last.

Your friend,
CHAS. F. LEWIS.

Chicago, Ill., Sept. 27.

My Dear Mr. Lewis:

Thanks for your advice and also thank your fiance for her generosity in allowing you to continue your correspondence with her "rivals," but personly I have no desire to take advantage of that generosity as I have something better to do than read letters from a man like you, a specially as I have a man friend who is not so generous as Miss Sears and would strongly object to my continuing a correspondence with another man. It is at his request that I am writing this note to tell you not to expect to hear from me again.

Allow me to congratulate you on your engagement to Miss Sears and I am sure she is to be congratulated too, though if I met the lady I would be tempted to ask her to tell me her secret, namely how she is going to "run wild" on $60.

Sincerely,
MABELLE GILLESPIE.